Dempsey and Makepeace
THE JERICHO SCAM

Also available from Futura

JOHN RAYMOND

Dempsey and Makepeace
THE JERICHO SCAM

Based on an original screenplay
by Jeffrey Caine

Futura

Chapter

ONE

The car taking Dempsey and Makepeace to the church was a white, chauffeur-driven Rolls Royce. It was gliding like a phantom through the grey, rain-spattered streets of Islington, North London, and pedestrians couldn't help staring at it as it went past.

Dempsey, wearing an immaculate morning suit, peered out the window and muttered, 'Jeez, look at that rain. What a great day for a wedding.'

'It's not the weather that's worrying me,' said Makepeace, glancing at her watch. 'It's whether we're going to arrive on time. We're cutting it very close.'

'Relax. They can't start without the Best Man and the . . . er, Best Lady?'

'Maid of Honour.'

'Whatever.' He gave her an admiring look. 'You know, you look kind of . . . okay.' She was dressed in a powder-blue gown of a simple, classical design and with a plunging, v-shaped neck-line.

'And you look like you're on the way to a Mafia funeral,' she told him.

'Gee, thanks,' he said, sounding hurt. 'You pay someone a compliment and they kick sand in your face. What's eating you?'

'Nothing,' she said curtly.

Dempsey shrugged and returned his attention to the passing, rain-soaked scenery. After drumming his fingers idly on the arm rest for a while he said, 'Can you figure it. Ol' Chas getting hitched?'

'Why is that so surprising?' she asked him.

'Well, I thought Chas had more smarts than that. I mean, marriage is for the birds.'

Makepeace gave him a hard stare. 'Just because you made a mess of *your* marriage doesn't mean there's anything wrong with the institution of marriage. It just says something about you.'

He frowned at her. 'Hey, you sure are prickly today. Why are you suddenly so touchy on the subject of marriage?'

'Mind your own business.'

'You thinking of getting married, princess? Chas and Mary's wedding got you all gooey on the idea? If you like, we can make it a double wedding.'

'Oh, shut up.' She turned her face to the window.

Dempsey looked puzzled for a few moments then grinned knowingly. 'Let me guess, princess. Your Lord Fauntleroy has proposed, am I right?'

A red spot appeared on Makepeace's cheek. Her gaze still fixed on the window she said, 'I've told you before not to call him that. His name is Nigel Penward.'

'Yeah, but he *is* a Lord, isn't he?' asked Dempsey, enjoying himself.

'Not yet. He inherits the title when his father dies. At the moment he's just an Honourable.'

'An honourable? An honourable what?'

She sighed. 'Don't be obtuse, Dempsey. He is entitled to be addressed as the Honourable Nigel Penward.'

'You're kidding.'

Makepeace didn't respond.

Dempsey said, 'So anyway, did the *Honourable* Nigel pop the question?'

'As a matter of fact he did,' said Makepeace quietly.

'Oho!' laughed Dempsey. 'And what did he say when you turned him down flat?'

'I didn't.'

'You *what*?' cried Dempsey, aghast.

'I said I didn't turn him down. I said I'd think about it and tell him my answer in a week.'

Dempsey, genuinely shocked, exclaimed, 'Princess, are you crazy?! I know you've been seeing a lot of the guy recently but *marry* him? You're not going to tell me you're in love with that wimp . . .'

She turned to face him, eyes flashing with anger. 'Not one more word, Lieutenant! Just mind your business and keep your nose out of my private life . . .'

The chauffeur, aware that the atmosphere in the passenger compartment was quickly worsening, chose that moment to slide open the glass partition and say over his shoulder, 'Care for some music?' As he spoke the sound of light classical music issued forth from hidden speakers on either side of the rear seat. Makepeace said coldly, 'What we'd care for is for you to get a move on. We're going to be late.'

The chauffeur, a thin, sombre-looking man in his late forties, said, 'Strict company policy that we always keep to the speed limit, Miss. Be more than my job's worth to disobey the rules, especially in these conditions.'

Makepeace folded her arms and glared at the back of his neck.

Dempsey leaned forward and said to the chauffeur, 'Hey, that thing get FM?'

'Dempsey . . .' said Makepeace warningly.

'Hey, I like to keep in touch, you mind?'

'We're off-duty.'

'A good cop is never off-duty,' he told her sternly.

'Give me strength,' she murmured.

Not many blocks away, in the basement of a disused newspaper shop, two men were making good progress with a pickaxe and sledge hammer through the lower wall. They had already penetrated some six feet and Bert Simmons, the older of the two men, knew they didn't have much further to go.

Ian Phelps, his young partner, said loudly, 'Almost time for the results of the 2.30 at Newmarket. Okay if I turn on the radio, Mr Simmons?'

'No, no, don't stop. Keep digging! We don't have much time.'

'But I got a tenner on "Duchess of Malfi" in that race,' protested Phelps.

'You punters . . .' gasped Simmons, the sweat rolling down his round, red face from all the exertion. 'Always after easy money.'

'Not like you, eh, Mr Simmons?'

'Look, I'm in trouble, son, or I wouldn't be doing this. It wouldn't be worth the risk normally.'

''ere!' said Phelps. 'You told me this job would be a doddle! You didn't say nothing about no risks!'

'Son,' said Simmons and paused as he swung the pickaxe into the concrete. '. . . Robbing a bank is *always* risky.'

At that moment the point of his pickaxe penetrated the bank vault. At the same time the pickaxe also broke a hair-thin wire; part of network covering the inner wall of the vault.

'That's it — you got it!' cried Dempsey as the chauffeur finally succeeded in tuning into the police wave band.

'Is this what you do when you're off-duty?' asked Makepeace irritably. 'Listen to police messages?'

'Doesn't everyone?'

'I cer . . .'

'Shush!' he cried. 'Listen . . .'

'. . . I repeat, M.P. to all mobiles vicinity Archer Street,' came the terse voice over the radio, 'Go immediately to Frith and Hanway bank, 31 Archer Street. Robbery in progress . . .'

Dempsey turned and grinned triumphantly at Makepeace. 'See! That's only a coupla streets away . . .'

'So's the church. We've got a wedding to go to!'

'Hey, Chas will understand.'

'Understand? Dempsey, you're the Best Man. You've got the ring, remember?'

Dempsey frowned. 'Oh yeah.'

Chas was waiting anxiously in the driveway of the church. From inside the church came the strains of the organ. The ceremony was due to start but Dempsey and Makepeace had yet to arrive. He looked at his watch again. *Where the hell were they?*

Then, to his intense relief, he saw a white Rolls Royce coming down the street. As it turned into the driveway he ran forward to meet it, planning to shelter them with his umbrella as they got out but to his surprise the Rolls didn't stop. Instead it just slowed down a little and, through the open rear window, he saw Dempsey toss something towards him.

'Sorry, Pal. Explain later!' cried Dempsey, then the Rolls had done a U-turn and was back out in the street.

Chas's mouth was hanging open in astonishment. He watched disbelievingly as the Rolls disappeared down the street. Then he looked down. Lying by his feet was his gold wedding ring.

'He's never going to forgive us,' said Makepeace.

Dempsey wasn't listening. He was staring intently ahead, his Colt Cobra in his hand. Then he cried, 'That's them!' and pointed.

Two men were running out of a derelict newspaper shop next door to the Frith and Hanway bank. One of the men was about fifty and overweight, the other one was in his twenties. Both were carrying large sacks. They were heading towards a yellow Jaguar parked nearby.

As the Rolls pulled up Dempsey and Makepeace leapt out. 'Oh hell,' muttered Makepeace as she landed in a large, muddy puddle.

'Police!' yelled Dempsey. 'Freeze or I shoot!'

Both men kept running. The younger one, in the lead, reached the Jaguar and dived inside. Dempsey fired a shot into the air. The older man came to an abrupt halt, dropped his sack and put his hands in the air. But the Jaguar took off with a screech of burning rubber.

At that moment a police Panda car arrived. Dempsey grabbed the overweight man and hustled him towards the Panda. 'All yours, pal,' he told the young constable who was getting out of the patrol car.

Looking perplexed, the constable said, 'Just a minute — who are *you* . . .?'

Dempsey quickly flashed his S.I.10 indentification, then hurried back to the Rolls. 'Come on, move it!' he told Makepeace who was unsuccessfully trying to keep her wet hair out of her eyes.

As they climbed back into the Rolls, Dempsey said to the chauffeur, 'Follow that car!'

'Are you serious, sir?'

'Of course I'm serious! Step on it!'

The Rolls began to move but very slowly . . .

The two constables stood watching the white Rolls move at a funereal pace down the road. 'Bloody hell,' said the first one. 'They operate in a different world in S.I.10, don't they? Join with them and they supply you with a Rolls Royce and a blonde.'

'I think I'll put in for a transfer,' said the second constable wistfully.

'Hey, what about *me?*' complained Simmons. 'You gonna arrest me or what?'

'Will you put some speed on!' yelled Dempsey to the chauffeur. 'He's getting away!'

'I told you,' said the chauffeur huffily. 'I have to obey the speed limit. Company policy.'

'To hell with company policy! This is police business!'

'Company policy is company policy. It would be more than my job is . . .'

'I know, I know — more than your job is worth.

Stop the car!'

'You what?' asked the chauffeur.

'Stop the car!' exploded Dempsey.

The Rolls came to a halt. Dempsey leapt out, pulled open the driver's door and hauled the chauffeur out of his seat. 'I'm commandeering this car.'

'You can't do that!' protested the chauffeur.

'Watch me.' Dempsey got in and slammed the door. Seconds later the Rolls was moving off at high speed. 'You see which way that Jag went?' Dempsey asked Makepeace over his shoulder.

'It took the second turning on the right . . .'

Dempsey put his foot down. Then, as he approached the turning he called, 'Hang on, princess . . .'

The Rolls skidded across the road as Dempsey executed a tight turn at speed. From the back Makepeace said, with alarm, 'Dempsey, you dingbat, take it easy! That chauffeur was right. The roads are very slippery today.'

'I know what I'm doin'. Just sit back and enjoy the ride.'

Up ahead he saw the yellow Jaguar taking another fast corner. Its driver, he realized, was a skilful one. 'The guy's good!' he told Makepeace. 'But I'm better . . .!'

'Dempsey . . .' said Makepeace warningly as he approached the corner without slowing. 'Be care . . .'

It was too late. As Dempsey swung the wheel sharply the Rolls went into a skid and this time Dempsey wasn't able to regain control.

Makepeace gave a screech of alarm as the Rolls went skidding sideways along the road, narrowly missing a double decker bus coming in the opposite direction, then mounted the pavement and went

12

hurtling towards a glass shop-front.

Dempsey jammed his foot down hard on the brake pedal but it was no use. The white Rolls Royce crashed through the shop window and only came to a halt when it rammed into a wall of shelving containing rows of paint tins.

The shelving collapsed and suddenly the white Rolls Royce was no longer white.

From within the wreckage of her expensive hair-do Makepeace moaned, 'Brilliant, Dempsey. Of all the shops available you have to crash into a *paint* shop.'

He pounded the steering wheel with his fist. 'Lousy goddamn British cars!' he growled.

· Chapter

TWO

'... And here's the bill from the car hire company,' said Makepeace as she handed the piece of paper across Spikings' desk. His eyes bulged when he read the total. 'I could *buy* a Rolls Royce for that much!' he roared.

Makepeace flinched.

'I absolutely refuse to authorise payment on this! It's totally out of order ...!'

'Er, sir,' said Makepeace hesitantly, 'I don't think you have any choice. After all, Dempsey did commandeer the car for police business. And he was driving it on said police business when we crashed into the ...' Makepeace paused.

'Paint shop.'

She nodded. 'Paint shop.'

Spikings looked at the bill again and glowered. 'Why did he have to choose a *paint* shop?'

'I asked exactly the same question, sir.'

'And how am I going to explain this to the top brass? One of my men commandeers a Rolls Royce that's supposed to be taking him to a wedding and goes haring off after a bank robber in it ... and in the process wrecks the car as well as giving it an all-the-colours-of-the-rainbow paint job?!'

'It will be difficult,' agreed Makepeace.

'Difficult? It'll be bloody impossible!!' he roared.

Makepeace maintained a diplomatic silence.

'So where's America's answer to Stirling Moss now?' asked Spikings.

She hesitated before answering. 'He's gone to H. Division at Holborn. Simmons, the man we grabbed, was taken there and Dempsey wants to question him.'

Spikings made a sound at the back of his throat and his complexion went from red to puce. Finally he managed to get the words out: 'He's gone ... where? To do *what*?'

'Well, it was *our* collar, sir ...' said Makepeace, but not too loudly.

'I don't care whose it was — it's not S.I.10 business and you both know it! When Dempsey returns I want to see him right away. And when I'm finished with him you can come in with a brush and dust pan to collect the pieces.'

Dempsey was striding purposefully along a corridor deep within the bowels of Holborn Central when his path was suddenly blocked by a tall, lean man aged about forty-five and with a face that radiated aggression and arrogance in equal parts. 'And where do you think you're going?' he demanded of Dempsey.

Dempsey felt an immediate and instinctive dislike

for the man, and he guessed the feeling was mutual. 'Interview room,' he answered curtly. 'See a guy name of Simmons.'

'Oh, you are, are you? And just who might you be? Mike Hammer? Sam Spade? Philip Marlowe?'

Dempsey could already feel his temper start to strain at the leash. He struggled to keep it under control. 'Lieutenant Dempsey, sir. On special attachment to S.I.10.' He produced his ID and showed it to the man. 'The desk sergeant said it was okay to see Simmons.'

'Did he now? Well, for your information, *Loo*-tenant ...' said the man sarcastically, 'I'm the one who says what's okay around here. And what I say is it *isn't* okay. Okay?'

Dempsey stared hard at him, still struggling to keep his temper under control. 'Let me take a wild guess — you're the head honcho around here, right?'

'I'm Detective Chief Inspector Lacey, Divisional C.I.D. And you address me as "sir". Understand? Or shall I go and fetch an interpreter?'

'Come on, don't give me a hard time ... sir,' said Dempsey brusquely. 'I already got clearance from Division. I got an interest in this guy. I'm the arresting officer.'

'I know what *you* are, *Loo*-tenant. You're a cowboy. I've heard about you, Dempsey, and I certainly don't want you in my territory.'

'You telling me to get out of town, sir?' asked Dempsey, straight-faced.

'I'm telling you that I don't like cowboys like you. So I'm warning you not to step out of line with me or I'll come down on you like a ton of bricks. Understand?'

'I reckon I get the message, sheriff,' drawled

Dempsey. 'Now do you mind if I go do the job I came here to do?'

Lacey's eyes blazed with anger. 'You say you've got clearance from Division?'

'Yeah,' lied Dempsey, hoping Lacey wouldn't check up.

'Very well ... but don't take too long. The sooner you're out of here the happier I'll be.' Lacey strode off, trailing black clouds of ill-feeling behind him.

'There's a stage leaving town at noon. Be under it,' muttered Dempsey under his breath as he continued on towards the Interview Room.

Simmons was sitting at the bare, plastic-topped table. He looked up as Dempsey entered. His expression was one of weary defeat. Dempsey had encountered a lot of robbers in his time, including a lot of bank robbers, but this man definitely did not fit the type.

He sat down opposite Simmons and gave him a friendly grin. 'How ya doin'?'

'How do you expect? I'm jumping for joy. Always do that when I get arrested.' He frowned at Dempsey. 'And I recognise you. You're the one who nicked me. Except you're not dressed so formally now. Didn't know what to think when you jumped out of that white Rolls Royce waving that cannon. Thought I was losing my marbles ...'

Dempsey gave an embarrassed cough and said, 'I did some checking on you. You run a lumber yard. So what's a guy in the lumber business doing robbing banks?'

'Robbing *a* bank, not banks. But like you say, I'm in lumber. Dead lumber.'

'British joke, right? I'll laugh later. After you

17

answer my question.'

'What can I say? It seemed a good idea at the time.'

'Yeah? You're sitting in your office and you say to yourself, "Gee, the lumber business is a little quiet today. Maybe I'll go catch a movie. No, I know what. I'll go rob a bank." Is that how it happened? Like a sudden whim?'

Simmons managed a weak smile. 'Something like that, yeah.'

'You're in deep trouble, you know that, don't you?'

He sighed. 'Your colleagues here have already pointed that fact out to me.'

'I can help you.'

'Yeah?' asked Simmons, disinterestedly.

'I mean it.'

Simmons shrugged. 'Your game, Yank. You deal ...'

'You give me the name of the other guy — your wheel man — and I'll put in a word for you with the judge.'

'He got away did he? I thought so. I asked but they wouldn't tell me here.'

'Yeah, he got away, and he got up my nose as well. So how about it?'

Simmons was about to answer, then paused and looked thoughtful. Then he said slowly, 'He's small beer. Just a stupid kid and I'm not going to grass on him, but ... but suppose I gave you something else?'

'Like what?'

'Like something different. Bigger. Much bigger.'

Dempsey leaned forward in his chair. 'I'd be interested.'

'When I say it's big I mean it. I'd need protection.'

'Something being planned?'

Simmons shook his head. 'It's already been done.'

'Yeah? So give.'

'I want your word. Your personal word.'

'You got it,' Dempsey assured him.

But before Simmons could say anything else the door suddenly opened and in stepped Chief Inspector Lacey followed by an impeccably dressed man carrying an expensive-looking briefcase.

'On your horse, cowboy,' Lacey told Dempsey with a sneer. The other man, ignoring Dempsey, smiled at Simmons and extended his hand. 'Nigel Armitage, Mr Simmons. Of Endicott, Drake and Armitage. We'll be representing you.'

Simmons, looking confused, shook his hand.

'Did you hear what I said, cowboy?' said Lacey. 'On your horse.'

The solicitor finally acknowledged Dempsey's presence. He raised a thin eyebrow and said, 'You are . . . ?

'He's nobody,' answered Lacey.

'*Lieutenant* Nobody,' Dempsey told the solicitor. 'S.I.10.'

A flicker of concern appeared in the solicitor's eyes then quickly vanished. 'My client has nothing to say to you, Lieutenant.' he said smoothly.

Dempsey turned to Simmons, 'You want to talk to me you go ahead. He can't stop you.'

'But *I* can,' said Lacey angrily before the worried-looking Simmons could reply. 'I checked with your chief. You don't have any authorisation from Division. He doesn't want you here and neither do I. So out, before I have you thrown out.'

Dempsey slowly got up. Ignoring both Lacey and Armitage he grinned at Simmons and said, 'Okay, we'll talk another time. See ya, pal.' Then he walked out.

But Lacey followed him into the corridor. 'I'm warning you, cowboy, keep your nose out of this case! It doesn't concern you.'

Dempsey kept on walking down the corridor.

'I need my head examined,' said Makepeace.

'Gwmph,' said Dempsey. He was busily devouring a large hot dog dripping with tomato sauce and mustard. Makepeace winced and looked away. They were sitting in Dempsey's car which was parked in a side street in Kentish Town. Further along the street was an ageing yellow Ford van with the sign "J.M. SIMMONS, BUILDERS MERCHANTS" painted on its sides. Simmons himself was in a nearby phone booth. He'd been in there for a considerable time.

'I mean, it's ridiculous,' continued Makepeace. 'Spikings is baying for your blood and what do you do? You call me up and ask me to help you on a stake-out. An *unofficial* stake-out on the very man Spikings wants you to leave alone. I don't need this, Dempsey. I really don't.'

'Gwmph,' said Dempsey. Then he offered her a bite out of his hot dog. She made a face. 'Oh, sorry,' he said and turned the hot dog round so that he was now offering her the uneaten end.

Makepeace grimaced. 'Please don't point that thing at me. Take it away before I get ill.'

He looked surprised. 'Hey, it's good! Best I've had since I've been in this country.'

'I'm not a hot dog sort of woman, Dempsey,' she informed him coolly. 'You must have noticed that by now.'

Simmons, still in the phone box, glanced towards them over his shoulder and frowned.

20

'This is something new in stake-out procedure,' she said. 'Making sure that the subject is aware that we're watching him.'

'I'm trying to make him edgy. He won't talk to me now. I hung around Holborn Central after Lacey threw me out. I see him come out with his slick lawyer. They shake hands and go their separate ways. I follow Simmons, catch up with him and tell him to spill what he was about to spill in the Interview Room but he refuses. Acts all worried and says he's changed his mind about making a deal. I wanna know why he's clammed up and I'm gonna stick on his tail until I do.'

'Did he give you any idea of what the job was that he was going to tell you about?'

'Nope. Only that it had already happened and that it was big. Very big.'

'Well, it *had* to be big,' Makepeace said as she looked again at the computer read-out on Simmons. 'After all, what we have here is a right little Napoleon of crime. Two illegal parkings, one Drunk in Charge and one Disorderly Conduct. At Christmas in 1965. That's a record sheet that would make Al Capone green with envy.'

'Go ahead, mock.'

She folded up the computer print-out. 'Dempsey, the man is practically a model citizen. Apart from a tendency to get drunk at Christmas and one little bank robbery he's Mr Clean.'

'Yeah. That's why it's fishy. Why does a guy like that suddenly decide to knock off a bank?'

'He needs the money. His business is in a bad way. He's facing bankruptcy . . .'

'I know, I *know*, but it still doesn't figure that the first thing a guy like Simmons picks on to raise some

21

cash is a bank job.'

'Seems perfectly sensible to me, Dempsey.'

'Yeah? Well, I got this feeling in my gut . . .'

'That's the hot dog.'

At that moment Simmons finally came out of the phone booth. He glanced, frowning, at them then got into his van and drove off. Dempsey immediately started his motor.

'You're getting obsessive again. I recognize the signs,' said Makepeace as Dempsey pulled away from the kerb.

'I gotta hunch. A strong one. And it sure isn't the hot dog talking back.'

'You and your hunches.'

'Don't knock 'em. The last one I had saved your life, remember?'

'Well,' she said grudgingly, 'That was different.'

Before Dempsey could reply the two-way radio crackled into life.

'. . . Control to Charlie Five . . .'

Dempsey picked up the mike and depressed the SEND button. 'Charlie Five.'

'Charlie Five,' said the Controller, 'I have a message for you. You are to return immediately — repeat immediately — to headquarters and report to Chief Superintendent Spikings. Over.'

'Message received and understood. Over and out.' Dempsey replaced the mike and scowled. 'Great,' he muttered. 'Just great.'

'Can we stop at a florist on the way back?' asked Makepeace.

'A florist? Why?'

'So I can buy some flowers for your funeral.'

Chapter
THREE

'How'd you know we were tailing Simmons?' Dempsey asked Spikings.

'I'm a policeman.'

'Meaning what?'

'Meaning I was informed,' said Spikings coldly. He leaned back in his chair, his expression hard. 'Leave Simmons to Division, Dempsey. That's an order.'

'Informed? Can't you smell something? I can smell something. So can Makepeace.'

'Hey, don't bring my nose into this!' she protested. 'I can't smell anything.'

'Well, *I* can. I can smell Big Money. Power. Influence. Endicott, Drake and Armitage. Those guys are bigtime. They're corporation lawyers.'

In a low, ominous voice, Spikings said, 'Stay out of it.'

Dempsey stuck out his chin. 'And what if I don't?'

'You can start thinking about looking for a new occupation.'

Dempsey considered this for a few moments then nodded. 'Okay, I'll take that risk.'

Spikings stared at him for a long time. Finally in a softer tone of voice, he said, 'All I want to know — and this is genuine interest — is what's so fascinating about one dull little amateur bank robber that you'd risk your career over him, Dempsey?'

'Okay, Chief, you got me . . .'

'I know.'

Makepeace said, 'Actually, sir, there *is* something odd about this thing . . .'

'You keep out of it,' Spikings told her. 'Or your career will be on the line as well.'

'But she's right!' protested Dempsey. 'The guy's business goes kerflooie, next thing he's robbing banks.'

With exaggerated patience Spikings said, 'It happens. It happens all the time. It's called *crime*, Dempsey.'

Dempsey sighed. 'Sure. But why's a guy like *him* rob a bank? And why that bank?'

'It opens Saturdays.'

'I'm trying to be serious here, Chief. Simmons is broke, right? So who made bail for him? And who's payin' this megabuck attorney?'

'And will Gerald find out that Sid is the baby's real father?' said Spikings facetiously.

Ignoring him, Dempsey said, 'Someone — somewhere — is putting the pressure on . . .'

Spikings nodded.

Encouraged, Dempsey continued, 'Somebody big is calling the shots on this thing . . .'

'I agree,' said Spikings.

'You do?' Dempsey asked, surprised by this apparent change of heart.

'I do. And I know who.'

Both Dempsey and Makepeace waited expectantly. 'Yeah?' said Dempsey. 'Who?'

Spikings leaned forward across his desk and, after a long pause, suddenly thundered, 'ME!'

They both flinched. Spikings continued at the same glass-shattering volume. 'And you know what this big-shot is going to do?!' He pointed a quivering finger at Dempsey. 'He's going to order you to take a week's leave as of *now*!! Go home, Dempsey! Watch TV. Get drunk. Get laid. Do whatever you want but if I hear you're still sniffing around the Simmons case I shall arrange for your leave to be permanent! Understand?!'

Dempsey said slowly, 'Let me get this straight, Chief . . . you want me to lay off Simmons, right?' He turned to Makepeace. 'Is that what he's tryin' to tell me?'

Makepeace said nothing.

'Get out of my office,' said Spikings hoarsely. '*Now*.'

'How to win friends and influence people,' said Makepeace, as they returned to their own office. 'You really handled that well.'

'Somebody's leaning on him.'

'Who?'

'The Chief.'

'No. I mean who's leaning on *him*?'

Dempsey shrugged. 'Someone up the line. One of the heavy guns at Division.'

'Well, even if you're right there's not much you can do about it. Have a nice holiday, Dempsey.'

Dempsey grunted something as he sat down at his

desk. He began leafing through a phone book. Then he picked up his phone and quickly punched out a number.

'Who are you calling?' Makepeace asked him.

'Shush.' Then, into the phone, he said urgently, 'I wanna speak to Mr Endicott. It's an emergency. My name? Wayne. James Wayne. What's it about? I wanna *hire* him, that's what it's about. I just got busted on a drugs charge and I need a good lawyer. No, I need the *best* lawyer ...' He paused, listening. Then, in an aggrieved tone, said, 'You got to be kidding, lady. Could you repeat that?'

He held the phone out towards Makepeace. She put her ear to the ear-piece and heard a woman with a cut-glass accent say, 'I said I'm sorry Mr Wayne but this firm does not take instructions in criminal cases. Someone has obviously misinformed you ...'

Dempsey hung up and gave Makepeace a triumphant look. 'What did I tell ya?'

'Fishy, Mr Wayne. Very fishy.'

'I think I'll go pay a visit to the bank.'

'Dempsey, you're on leave.'

'So I'm on leave. So in my spare time I wanna go see a bank. Is that a crime?'

'No. It's an act of suicide if Spikings finds out.'

He shrugged. 'I'll take that risk. You wanna come along?'

'Why should I risk my career as well?'

'Because you're just as curious as I am. Admit it.'

She sighed and nodded. 'I suppose we lemmings have got to stick together.'

When they arrived back at the bank with its adjoining shop they found it a hive of activity. There was a sand lorry and large cement mixer parked outside and several workmen in evidence. Dempsey pulled up behind the cement mixer and they got out. One of the workmen gave Makepeace a wolf whistle and she glowered at him.

'Easy, princess,' murmured Dempsey. 'Take it as a compliment.'

'Compliment my eye!' she replied angrily. 'You know as well as I do what it was.'

Dempsey shrugged and led the way towards the entrance of the shop. As they passed the sand lorry he pointed out the name on its side. 'Harris-Strang ... who are they?'

'Just about the biggest building contractors in London.'

'Yeah? What are they doing fooling around with a penny-ante job like this?'

'Banks have money. When they're not being robbed, that is.'

They entered the shop and went downstairs. The cement wall had already been replaced and plasterers were at work on the damaged ceiling.

'These guys work fast,' commented Dempsey as he stared at the fresh cement.

'I told you, they're the best.'

One of the plasterers came over to them. 'Oi! What's your game? What are you doin' here?'

Dempsey produced his ID. The plasterer was not impressed. 'Too late, mate.' He pointed at the door. 'They went thataway a long time ago.'

The other plasterers roared with laughter.

'You'd better get moving then,' continued the first man. 'But you can leave blondie here if you like. We'll take good care of her 'til you get back.'

Makepeace stiffened. Dempsey said quickly,

27

'Blondie here happens to be a cop like me so watch your mouth.'

The plasterer made a show of appearing apologetic. Smirking, he tugged at his forelock in mock deference, and said to Makepeace, 'Oh, sorry, ma'am. Please don't arrest me, ma'am ...'

Again came the guffaws of laughter from the other plasterers. Dempsey glared at them then said, 'Come on, let's get out of here before the keeper comes to feed these monkeys ...'

As they re-emerged into the street Makepeace said, 'Don't worry, Dempsey. They were just paying me a compliment.'

'Okay, Okay, I get your point,' he growled.

'Good. But what I don't get is the point of our visit here. What were you looking for down there?'

He rubbed his chin. 'Dunno ... something.'

'*Something*? What kind of something?'

'I don't know yet. But something doesn't jell ...'

'Well, that's a big help. We're looking for a "something" that doesn't jell. Can't be many of those around.'

'They give you a diploma when you majored in sarcasm?'

'All right, to be serious for a moment we need more to go on than one of your famous hunches.'

'I know,' he sighed. 'But right now that's all I got.'

As they returned to their car they didn't notice the man sitting in the red Land Rover parked across the street. He was in his early forties and had the face of someone who gets into fights for the fun of it and rarely comes off second best. When Dempsey and Makepeace had driven off he picked up his car phone and rapidly punched a number ...

Lacey fixed Simmons with an icy stare. 'If it's here we'll find it, Simmons. Lot better for you if you save us the trouble.'

Simmons shrugged and said easily, 'You find any money in this place, you can keep it.'

Lacey turned to his companion, Detective Sergeant Taylor, a dour-faced thirty year old, and said, 'Hear that, Taylor? Attempting to bribe a police officer.'

Taylor nodded sombrely.

Simmons raised his eyes to the ceiling of his office. 'It was a joke, officer. Just a joke.'

'Bank robbery is no joke,' intoned Lacey. 'And if you don't come to your senses and start cooperating you're going to be in even bigger trouble. Now let me ask you again — where did your mate stash his share of the proceeds?'

'And I'll tell you again, officer, that I have no idea! The lad and I were going to go our separate ways after the job. He wouldn't have come here with his money. He knew I got nicked. He'd have to be a real mug to hide cash in my yard after that, wouldn't he?'

'Not necessarily,' said Lacey. 'He might figure it was the last place anyone would look.'

'Gordon Bennett!' muttered Simmons. 'Look the lad is probably halfway to Spain by now. We weren't close mates or anything. He's got no reason to stick around here. I only just met him a week ago.'

'How?'

Simmons hesitated. 'Er, he was recommended, like.'

'For the bank job?'

Simmons nodded.

'If he wasn't a close mate then there's no reason why you can't tell us his name. Is there, Taylor?'

'No reason at all,' said Taylor.

'I can't,' protested Simmons. 'You know I can't.'

Lacey leaned over Simmons' desk. 'Listen, we've got you cut and dried. Your average kipper has nothing on you. You're going to prison and all the fancy lawyers in the world aren't going to change that fact. Your only chance is to cooperate with me. I want some names. You give them to me or you're on your own.'

Simmons wore the expression of a man faced with the choice of plunging either his left hand or right hand into boiling water. 'You don't understand ... there's someone big involved and if ...'

'His name,' said Lacey. 'Now.'

Simmons was about to reply when he was interrupted by the sound of a car entering his lumber yard. 'Damn!' muttered Lacey and went to the window. His anger increased when he saw who was driving the car. 'Dempsey.'

'Lacey,' said Dempsey bitterly when he recognised the face peering at him through the office window.

'Looks like a real mutual admiration society,' observed Makepeace as they got out of the car.

'Nah, don't get me wrong. I think he's a real fun guy.'

'He's a real fun Detective Chief Inspector.'

Dempsey stopped and looked at her. 'That a problem for you?'

'To be honest, yes. One day you'll be breezing back to the Big Apple full of tales about quaint little old England to your cronies back there. Trouble is I live in this quaint little old country. I have to work here. I don't need enemies in high places.'

He grinned. 'You can always come back to New

York with me, princess.'

'I'm serious.'

His grin vanished. 'Fine. Go wait in the car.'

'Don't tell me what to do.'

'Okay. Don't wait in the car.'

He continued walking. After a few seconds' hesitation Makepeace followed. 'Just so long as we understand one another, Lieutenant,' she said.

Lacey pointed at Dempsey as he and Makepeace entered Simmons' office. 'You, cowboy, are in big trouble . . .'

'Hey, calm down, your worshipfulness,' said Dempsey cheerfully. 'Me and Calamity Jane are here on legitimate business. Aren't we, Jane?'

Makepeace's cheeks flamed but she said nothing.

'You're lying,' Lacey accused him. 'I know for a fact your chief has put you on leave. You have absolutely no right to be here on police business.'

Dempsey contrived to look innocent. 'Who said anything about police business? I said I was here on *legitimate* business . . .' He turned and smiled at Simmons. 'Hi there. Whaddyahear-whaddyaknow?'

Simmons gave him an affable nod. 'Nothing to say, Lieutenant. Not to anyone.' He glanced meaningfully at Lacey.

'Well,' said Dempsey, 'What I want is, er . . . twenty-six feet of planed two-by-one . . . no knots . . . and one eight-by-four sheet of . . .'

'Right. That's it. Out!' cut in Lacey.

Dempsey looked surprised. 'Hey, can't a man buy some wood in this country? I'm building a doghouse. For my dog.'

'Don't treat me as a fool, Dempsey,' snarled Lacey. 'You know as well as I do that Simmons has ceased trading. He went to the wall . . .'

'We heard he went through it,' said Makepeace and gave Lacey a sweet smile.

He glared at her. 'Who the hell are you?'

'Sergeant Harriet Makepeace. S.I.10,' she told him.

'Well unless you want to be *Constable* Makepeace you'd better take this cowboy out of my sight ... *now!*'

Dempsey held up his hands. 'It's okay, marshal, I'm a'leavin' ... come on Calamity, before he sets his posse on us ...'

Out in the yard Makepeace said, 'Now I understand why you don't like him. He's a real creep. But you could have been more diplomatic with him ...'

'I'm a cop, not a diplomat. I'm trying to do a job and he's getting in my way.'

'He obviously feels the same thing about you.'

'Yeah, but I know what I'm doing.'

'Really? That's news to me. So what's your next move?'

Dempsey looked at his watch. 'Eat,' he said. 'I heard a new American hamburger place has opened in the Kings Road. Supposed to be almost the real thing. How about we go check it out? My treat.'

She shook her head. 'Sorry. I've got to go home and cook. I've got company coming tonight.'

'Lord Fauntleroy?'

She didn't answer.

Chapter
FOUR

'You look beautiful,' said Nigel Penward as he handed Makepeace a single red rose and bottle of Dom Perignon.

'So do you,' said Makepeace. 'Come in ...'

The Honourable Nigel Penward was a tall, slim man in his late thirties. His aristocratic good looks were marred only by his chin which, while it couldn't be described as receding, lacked a certain substance. He was wearing a charcoal grey Saville Row suit, a striped blue and white shirt and had a red carnation in his button hole.

Makepeace took his overcoat and hung it in the closet. 'Busy day?' she asked.

'Absolutely hellish,' he said as he sank gratefully into an armchair. 'The stock market has, as they say, got the jitters. All down to the falling oil prices, thanks to those bloody Arabs ...'

'What would you like to drink?' she asked him.

'Oh, a G & T would be heaven, darling . . .'

After putting the red rose in a vase and the champagne in the refrigerator Makepeace mixed two gin and tonics. As she was handing Penward his drink he took hold of her arm, indicating that she should lean forward to be kissed. She did so. Afterwards he said, 'God, you smell as lovely as you look. How was *your* day?'

'Oh, the usual,' she said as she went and sat down. 'Lots of running around without actually achieving anything. And, again as usual, watching Dempsey wage a one-man war against authority. Which he's losing, of course.'

'I don't know why you put up with that man,' said Penward. 'You should ask for a change of partner. Someone you'd be more compatible with.'

'Oh, he's all right really,' she said defensively. It's just that he's so . . . so , well, *American,* I suppose.'

He frowned. 'I still don't understand what a Yank cop is doing over here in our police force . . .'

'Well, it's a rather convoluted story but if you want to hear it . . .'

He waved a hand dismissively. 'Not really. The less I hear about him the better. Anyway, it's all academic now . . . As soon as we're married you can put all that police nonsense behind you.'

Makepeace bridled. 'It's not nonsense. It's my *career.*'

'It's no career for someone like you, darling. Besides, you told me you wanted to have children . . .'

'Well, yes, I do — I think — but not *yet.* Besides, I haven't even accepted your proposal. I told you I'd give you my answer within a week.'

'Oh, come on Harriet darling, you know what your answer is going to be, just as I do. My one regret is that we didn't do it ages ago. We had the chance, at Cambridge, but we blew it, didn't we?'

She raised an eyebrow. '*We* blew it? You went off with Lady Samantha Forbes-Knight. To Italy. I was absolutely shattered.'

For a moment he looked disconcerted but then his expression cleared and he said, 'Ah, but you became involved with that chap whatsisname — the one you married. The solicitor chap . . .'

'Robert. Robert Makepeace. And that was a whole year after you left me.'

He grimaced, took a swallow of his drink and said, 'Look, let's not talk about the past anymore. I'm just so thankful we ran into each other at Gstaad last month after all these years.'

'We didn't run into each other, we collided on the ski slope. That's always been your ploy for picking up women at ski resorts — you first knock them over . . .'

'I say, you don't think I *deliberately* . . .'

'Oh, you didn't know it was *me.* In fact you ought to have seen the look on your face when I took off my goggles. The bit of stuff you hoped to pick up turned out to be your old flame from university days . . .'

He gave an embarrassed cough. 'You've got me wrong, Harriet, I assure you.'

She smiled at him, enjoying his discomfort. 'On the contrary, I've got you right. You're a rogue, Nigel, which is probably why I like you so much. I've always had a soft spot for rogues . . .'

He smiled back at her.

After dinner, which consisted of oven-baked sole stuffed with lobster, shrimp and crab followed by strawberries and cream, they opened another bottle of champagne and retired to the couch. Makepeace was feeling very good — and very romantic. She accepted his embrace eagerly and kissed him with mounting passion . . .

Then the doorbell rang.

They pulled apart and stared at each other. 'Are you expecting anyone?' Penward asked her.

'Of course not,' she replied. The bell sounded again. Reluctantly she got up and went to the door.

It was Dempsey. 'Hi babe,' he said, as she opened the door. 'Grab your coat, I need some help.' He pushed past her and bounded into the living room. Then he saw Penward on the sofa. 'Oh, hi pal . . . you must be, er . . .'

'This is Nigel Penward, Dempsey,' said Makepeace coldly. 'Nigel, meet James Dempsey, of whom you've heard so much.' Dempsey offered his hand to Penward who gave it a perfunctory shake. 'You know what,' said Dempsey. 'You're the second Nigel I've met today.'

'Really? How interesting,' said Penward stiffly.

'Yeah. And you're both very alike . . . it's kinda weird.'

'*Dempsey*, what are you *doing* here?' Makepeace demanded.

'I told you. I need you help . . .'

'And I told *you* that I was having company tonight! You can't just burst in like this and expect me to drop everything and go off with you!'

'Hey, Makepeace, it's police work! A good cop is never off duty, right?'

'Well *this* one is,' she said, tapping her chest. 'So please leave. Now.'

'I thought you wanted to know what the real story was behind the Simmons case.'

36

'I do, but . . .'

'But you're not willing to get your hands a little dirty, huh?' he said sadly. 'Princess, I'd never have figured you for a fair weather cop, you know?'

'Fair weather cop?' she replied indignantly. 'How dare you . . .?'

He held up his hands. 'It's okay. I'm goin'. You have a good night. Drink some more champagne . . .' He headed for the door.

Makepeace, her face twisted with indecision, said, 'Wait, Dempsey . . .'

He stopped at the door and turned. 'Yeah?'

Makepeace gave a long sigh. 'I'll come with you, damn you.'

Penward looked stunned. 'Darling, you're not actually *going* with this . . . this . . .'

Dempsey looked at him. 'This *what*, pal? Spit it out.'

Penward reddened. 'If you must know I was going to say, "this ill-mannered American boor",' he said coldly.

'Boar? You mean you're calling me a pig?'

'Not boar, *boor*. It means someone who is ill-bred. A peasant.'

'Yeah, well let me tell you, buddy, that . . .'

'Shut up the pair of you,' said Makepeace hastily as she went to the closet. 'Dempsey, are we going or not?'

'Sure. Let's go.' With a final angry glance at Penward, Dempsey opened the door. Makepeacè, slipping on an overcoat, said to Penward, 'I'll try to be as quick as I can, darling. Finish the champagne, if you like . . .'

'Yeah, pal, finish the champagne,' Dempsey told him as he shut the door.

37

Penward stared at the closed door and then muttered a single, succinct word. Then he repeated it.

'You can't really be serious about marrying that guy,' said Dempsey as he pulled away from the kerb.

'I don't want to discuss it,' she said firmly.

'But princess, he looks like a gigolo. I'm telling you the guy is a creep ... and I've seen fish with better chins than his.'

'Dempsey, for the last time, stay out of my private life.'

'I'm only trying to help you, kid. I'd do the same for any friend who was about to make a move that would ruin their entire life ...'

'Where are we going?' she asked through gritted teeth.

'Simmons' place. I wanna speak to him. Alone this time.'

'The lumber yard again?'

'No, his house. It's in Harrow.'

'Harrow! Oh no, that's miles away!'

'It won't take long.'

'Nigel is going to be furious.'

'Yeah. Poor Nigel.' Dempsey grinned.

Simmons lived in a modest, detached house in a quiet Harrow street called Greenleaf Lane. Dempsey parked the Mercedes on the opposite side of the road and surveyed Simmons' house. 'Must have bought that when his bank balance was a lot healthier,' he said.

'Don't sit there gawking. Get a move on.'

'I'll be five minutes. Count 'em.'

'Make the most of them, Dempsey. Because this is absolutely the last time . . .'

'I just want five minutes with the guy. Then we're off the case.'

'I mean it,' said Makepeace.

'So do I.' He opened his door then quickly shut it again. 'Hell!'

A car was coming out of Simmons' driveway. At first Dempsey couldn't see who was driving it but when it passed under the street light he saw that it was Simmons behind the wheel.

Dempsey and Makepeace crouched low as the headlights of Simmons' car swept over the Mercedes then they watched it head up the road. 'Dammit,' muttered Dempsey.

'I really love your timing tonight. That's the second time you've arrived at just the wrong moment.'

Dempsey got out of the car. 'Follow him, will ya, Harry? Be a pal.'

'What?'

'Go on, quick! Before you lose him!'

'And what are you going to be doing?'

'You don't wanna know.'

She slid angrily over into the driver's seat. 'You're right. I don't want to know.' She glared at him as she started the engine. He had to jump back to avoid having his toes run over as she took off after Simmons.

At the end of the street, under the shadow of a tree, was parked another car, a grey Ford Escort. There were two men in it. One of them was the same man who had observed Dempsey and Makepeace leaving the shop next to the bank that afternoon.

The two men watched Dempsey cross the road and go up to Simmons' front door. They saw him ring the doorbell then, after a short wait, disappear around the side of the house.

'He's being a bit of a naughty boy, eh, Mr Malley?' said the younger of the two men.

Malley nodded silently. Then he reached for the car phone.

Dempsey had no trouble in levering open a window at the side of the house. He climbed inside and found himself in the kitchen. Using a pen-sized flashlight Dempsey checked the rooms until he located Simmons' study. Then he proceeded to methodically and systematically search through Simmons' desk. It was a professional job in every respect except one — and which would later cause Dempsey a great deal of regret — he wasn't wearing any gloves . . .

Makepeace was talking to herself as she followed Simmons' car along the Harrow Road. '. . . Crazy, I must be crazy . . . here I am in a St Laurent dress trailing a third-rate amateur bank robber while at home I have a gorgeous man waiting for me . . . damn you, Dempsey . . .'

Then, over the police radio, she heard: 'M.P. to any mobiles vicinity of Greenleaf Lane. Go to 47 Greenleaf Lane. Repeat, 47 Greenleaf Lane. Intruder reported on premises. Suspected breaking and entering taking place . . .'

'*Double* damn you, Dempsey!' cried Makepeace.

She pulled up at the first phone box she encountered and quickly entered it. Simmons' car was rapidly disappearing into the distance but she didn't care. Getting in touch with Dempsey was the important thing now. She rapidly flipped through the directory, searching for Simmons' number . . .

Dempsey had found Simmons' bankbook. It made interesting reading. He was just turning over another page when the phone on the desk top started to ring. He froze, startled, and stared at it indecisively.

It kept ringing. On impulse he picked it up.

'Dempsey . . .?' He recognised Makepeace's voice but he didn't answer.

'Dempsey, I know it's you,' she said angrily. 'You just had to break in, didn't you? Cowboy style.'

He remained silent. He noticed a hardback book lying next to the phone. Idly, he began to leaf through it, then he looked again at its cover. The title read: Geology and Petrology of the Thames Valley.

'. . . The law doesn't apply to you, though, does it?' Makepeace continued in the same annoyed tones. 'You make me sick. You're smug, insensitive, bullish, arrogant, selfish, thoughtless . . .' Dempsey nodded, grinning to himself.

She paused for breath then went on: 'You think success justifies any dirty trick, don't you? Any violation of the rules, any breach of the civilised codes of conduct . . . Dempsey, you have the morality of a waste disposal unit and I have only one more thing to say to you . . .' She paused then said, 'There's a patrol car on its way to Simmons' house to arrest you.' Then she hung up.

Dempsey, taken by surprise, stared at the dead phone he was holding. Then, in the distance, he could hear the familiar sound of a police siren. And it was rapidly growing louder.

Chapter
FIVE

When Simmons drove into his lumber yard he saw a Rolls Royce parked outside his office. The office light was also on. He turned off his engine and sat there for a while, wishing he could go back in time and change some of the things that had happened during the past few days. Most of all he wished he could eradicate the moment when he decided to rob that bank.

With a resigned sigh he got out of his car and went into his office.

Seated behind his desk was a large, overweight man in his late fifties. He had a round, bland face but both his eyes and his thin lips revealed an underlying streak of cruelty that lay not far beneath the surface.

He smiled at Simmons and said almost jovially, 'Hello there, Simmons! Hope you don't mind me making myself at home like this ...'

'Not at all, Mr Harris,' said Simmons meekly.

Harris gestured at an empty chair with the large cigar

he was smoking. 'Sit down, Simmons, sit down. You look tired.'

Simmons sat down. 'I am. The last couple of days . . . well, you know . . .'

'I do,' nodded the fat man. 'Only too well.'

Simmons stared at him, trying to calculate his true mood behind this layer of superficial *bonhomie*. 'I could have made a run for it. But I didn't. I thought we could work it out. No reason for a problem. right?'

'None at all,' agreed Harris, knocking the ash off his cigar onto Simmons' desk top.

Simmons looked at the little pile of ash then into Harris's eyes. His feeling of nervousness increased. 'I mean, there are ways. No need for this to get out of hand.'

'I agree. Trouble is, Simmons, is that things have already got a bit out of hand.' He regarded Simmons with a sad expression. 'I paid you a good sum. But you had to knock off that bloody bank. Why?'

'I was desperate.'

Harris looked even sadder. 'There is desperate, my boy, and *desperate*. You have put everything I have in danger. My whole company, my organisation — everything that I have built up over the years — all because of a forty thousand quid bank job. And you couldn't even manage that without getting yourself nicked by a couple of passing off-duty cops. Now Simmons, I've been trying to put myself in your place — I have really — but I still can't understand why you did it.'

'I was stupid,' said Simmons in a defeated voice. 'What else can I say?'

Harris shook his large head. 'Nothing now. But you know I can't afford the risk of you going to court on this.'

The meaning of his words sunk into Simmons like

43

ice-cold knife blades. He suddenly felt very sick. 'Look, there's got to be a way out of this.'

'Can you think of one?' asked Harris, almost kindly. Simmon started to tremble.

'Tell me something,' said Harris. 'Was your life worth forty thousand quid?'

'Please ... I'm begging you ...'

'Did you say beg?' asked Harris, his eyes widening.

'I'll do anything ...'

There was the sound of a car entering the yard. Simmons stood up in alarm. 'Who ...?'

'Sit down,' said Harris calmly.

Simmons sat down. He listened nervously to the slamming of car doors and approaching footsteps. The office door opened and Simmons' heart sank even further. He only recognised one of the two men who entered the office but that was enough to confirm his worst fears. It was Bob Malley, Harris's main hard man — the one who did all his dirty jobs, and enjoyed doing them.

Malley grinned down at Simmons. ''Ullo, Mr Simmons. In a spot of bother, are we?'

The other man, a heavily-built skinhead in his late twenties, sniggered.

Simmons felt the sweat start to ooze down his collar which had suddenly become much too tight. 'You're ... going ... to kill me,' he told Harris accusingly.

Harris gave him a benign smile. 'No need for anything so drastic, lad. I think we can work this out.'

Hope flared through Simmons like the glow from a shot of whisky. 'We can? How? I told you, I'll do anything.'

Harris looked at Malley, then back at Simmons. 'This Yank, Dempsey, you're going to have to deal with him yourself.'

'You mean, you want me to ... to kill him?' asked Simmons shakily. 'I don't know if I can ...'

'No, no, you misunderstand me,' said Harris. 'I don't want anyone dead. Too dangerous. I just want this business buried, forgotten. Do you understand that?'

Simmons nodded, though he still didn't have any idea of just how that could be achieved.

'Malley knows what I have in mind, don't you Malley?' asked Harris.

'Sure, Mr Harris.'

'Then take Mr Simmons with you and explain the scheme to him now.'

'Right.' Malley stepped forward and put his huge hand on Simmons' shoulder. Simmons flinched and looked pleadingly towards Harris.

'You will cooperate with Malley, won't you? It's the only way we're going to be able to wipe the slate clean.'

Simmons gave an unwilling nod. He felt Malley's hand close around his upper arm. 'Come on, Mr Simmons, let's go.'

After one last pleading look at Harris, who just beamed back at him like a dissolute Buddha, Simmons got to his feet and allowed himself to be led out of the office ...

The first thing Dempsey did when he got back to his flat was to ring Makepeace. When she answered the phone she sounded annoyed. 'Oh, it's you. I thought you'd be behind bars by now.'

'Nah, no problem. I was in the car and moving before the patrol even turned into the street. Kid's play.'

'Pity,' said Makepeace.

'Hey, you sound pissed off. What's the matter? Lover-boy get too fresh with you or something?'

' "Lover-boy", as you describe him, was no longer here when I returned. He left a note saying he couldn't wait.'

'Tsk, tsk,' said Dempsey with mock sympathy. 'And you want to marry a guy who won't even hang around for you for just a couple of hours.'

'I don't blame him, Dempsey, I blame *you*. You ruined my whole evening.'

'Hey, look, you want me to come round and finish the champagne with you?'

'I certainly do not!'

He shrugged. 'Just tryin' to be helpful. So where'd Simmons go?'

'I wouldn't know. I had to stop and make an urgent phone call.'

'You mean you lost him? Is that what you're telling me? That you broke off a tail to make a goddamn phone call?'

'It seemed important at the time but in retrospect I'm having second thoughts about it,' she said coldly. 'Don't worry, it won't happen again.'

'You shoulda stayed with the tail.'

'Next time I will, believe me,' she said and then hung up.

Dempsey put down the phone with a sigh and wondered what his next move should be. No point in going back to Simmons' house again — the local police would probably be keeping an eye on the place after the 'break-in'. Besides, there was no guarantee that Simmons would be there. He might have gone for the night.

Dempsey was just fixing himself a scotch and soda when the phone rang. He presumed it was Makepeace ringing, perhaps to apologise but he was surprised to discover it was Simmons . . .

'You still ready for that talk, Lieutenant?' Simmons

asked him. He sounded nervous.

'Sure. Anytime. Anyplace.'

'Fine with me. Where?'

'You know where they're building that big new hotel? The Park Palace? In Princess Street down by the river?'

'Yeah, sure.'

'See you in half an hour then,' said Simmons and hung up.

It was quarter to one in the morning when Dempsey arrived at the hotel building site. He parked by the front gates and got out. The place was in darkness. All that could be heard was some plastic sheeting flapping in the cold wind. On the fence by the gates was a large Harris-Strang signboard. Next to it a smaller signboard warned that the site was patrolled by guard dogs.

Dempsey approached the gates and saw that they were unlocked — the heavy chain and padlock dangling open. He gave one of the gates a tentative push. It squeaked rustily inwards. He waited a few moments, listening for any sound of the dogs. Then he called, 'Simmons?! Simmons! It's me, Dempsey! I'm alone! Come out!'

There was no response. Dempsey drew his gun and squeezed in between the gates. Warily he looked around, expecting to see the dark shape of an Alsatian dog hurtling towards him at any second. But all remained still and quiet. The site seemed completely deserted.

He walked towards the base of the huge skeletal structure. The silence was beginning to get on his nerves. Where was Simmons? Had he chickened out? He'd certainly sounded scared on the phone ...

Then he heard a sound that made the hairs on the back of his neck stand up on end. It was a kind of high-pitched moaning. He paused, straining to see into the darkness. Then, in the shadow of one of the huts, he saw an outline on the ground. He moved cautiously towards it.

It was an Alsatian, whimpering in pain. Dempsey stood looking at it, not daring to get any closer to it. If he tried to stroke it, it would probably snap at him. 'It's okay, feller,' he said soothingly. 'Take it easy.' He felt helpless. The animal had obviously been poisoned.

Simmons? But why would Simmons want to poison it . . .?

He looked at the unfinished hotel again. It was not much more than a framework of girders stretching a very long way into the sky. Dempsey craned his neck to stare at the top — and then saw someone waving to him from the uppermost level. Simmons? There was only one way to find out . . .

Leaving the dying dog he hurried towards the base of the building. He soon found what he was looking for. It was next to a huge concrete mixer — the cage of the temporary construction elevator.

He got into the cage and used his pen torch to find the control panel. He pressed the UP button and far above him heard an electric motor come to life. With a jerk the cage began to rise.

Dempsey held onto the safety bar as the rudimentary elevator crawled up the side of the unfinished building. He felt too exposed and vulnerable . . .

Very soon he had a good view of the lights of London as the ground dropped further and further away. He shivered in the cold wind and began to wonder if coming here alone had been such a good idea.

Finally the elevator reached the top of the structure. Dempsey, gun in hand, stepped warily out onto a narrow wooden catwalk. There was no sign of Simmons now, or whoever it was who had beckoned to him.

He proceeded along the catwalk, trying not to look down. Normally heights didn't bother him but being on top of this incomplete, skeletal building made him feel very insecure. He couldn't help feeling that a foot in the wrong place might cause the whole insubstantial edifice to collapse beneath him.

'Simmons? Where the hell are you?' he called softly.

Then he heard a sound behind him. He started to turn but it was too late. Something hard slammed into his head just above his left ear. He tried to hang on to consciousness, knowing he *had* to if he wanted to stay alive, but it was no use. The lights of the city swirled and blurred before his eyes like a dissolve in a movie then disappeared completely. All that was left was the sensation of falling . . .

Dempsey woke up wondering why he'd left his bedroom window open on such a cold night. Shivering, he rolled over onto his side and reached out for the switch on his bedside-table lamp but his fingers met only empty air. He leaned further, and then found himself rolling off the edge of the bed . . .

Instinctively he made a grab for the bed as he fell. And saved his life. The discovery that the floor of his bedroom had apparently vanished snapped him back into full consciousness. It was then he became aware that he was dangling from a catwalk by his fingertips some three hundred feet above the ground.

Panic, combined with his powerful will to survive, gave him the strength to climb back onto the narrow catwalk. He lay there panting for a while then remembered what had happened ...

Someone had hit him from behind. It had been a set-up. They'd aimed to get rid of him. But why had they bungled the job? He'd been helpless ... so why hadn't they just dumped him over the side? He looked down and shuddered. Maybe they'd presumed he'd do the job himself, as he almost had ...

He took out his pen torch and shone it around. No one in sight but he did spot his Colt lying on the catwalk a few feet away. He went and picked it up. He checked the chamber: it was still loaded. He frowned ...

Then he became aware of something else. The sound of machinery coming from below. He looked over the edge again and saw that the big cement mixer was revolving.

Puzzled, he headed back to the elevator gantry. The cage wasn't there. He pressed the button, half expecting that nothing would happen but he heard the elevator start to rise.

On the way he tentatively felt the side of his head. There was a lump — a big one — but the skin wasn't broken, which suggested a blackjack.

When the elevator touched bottom he emerged cautiously from the cage. There didn't seem to be anyone in the vicinity of the rotating cement mixer but he didn't approach it directly; instead he made a wide circle around it before going nearer. He didn't intend being taken by surprise a second time that night.

Satisfied that no one was about he switched on his pen torch. He saw that the mixer had been used to pour fresh cement into a foundation trench very recently — the cement was obviously still wet. Then

50

he saw something else.

A hand.

It was sticking up out of the wet cement.

Dempsey quickly bent down beside the trench and began to claw the sludge-like cement away from around the hand . . .

Very soon he had uncovered part of a body, then the victim's face.

He wasn't too surprised when he saw it was Simmons.

Chapter
SIX

Dempsey's first thought when he discovered Simmons' corpse in the cement was to hurry back to his car and radio headquarters but then he realized that wouldn't be the wisest of moves. It would be difficult trying to explain to Spikings what he'd been doing at the site, especially as he'd had strict orders to stay off the Simmons case.

Instead, after a final check of the area, he returned to his car and drove to the nearest phone box. From there he made an anonymous 999 call, using a handkerchief over the mouthpiece and doing his best to fake a British accent, and told the New Scotland Yard operator where Simmons' body could be found. Then he went home.

After taking three aspirin and fixing a cold compress for his head Dempsey sat down with a large scotch and soda and tried to think things out. He mentally ticked off the facts as he knew them, trying to build up an overall picture of the situation. Fact one: whoever had killed Simmons was the 'somebody' big in Simmons' background. Simmons knew too much and had to be eliminated. Fact two: the same person had set Dempsey up by getting Simmons to call him and arrange a meeting. Fact three: the aim of the set-up was not to murder Dempsey as well but to somehow implicate him in Simmons' death. That way the mystery 'Mr Big' would kill two birds with one stone. Fact four: the plan hadn't worked. There was no way Dempsey could be connected with Simmons' death . . .

He wondered what to do next. With Simmons gone his line of enquiry had come to an apparent dead end. Unless . . . unless his missing getaway driver turned up. But fat chance of that, thought Dempsey disgustedly. The guy was probably out of the country by now . . .

Ian Phelps was dredged out of a deep sleep by a persistent knocking on the door of the Earls Court bedsit he was hiding out in. He sat up and switched on his bedside lamp. 'Shit,' he muttered when he saw the time. It was 4.30 in the morning.

He got out of bed and, shivering, went to the door. 'Who is it?' he called through it.

'It's Malley,' came the reply. 'Open up. I got to talk to you.'

Phelps experienced a stab of fear. What the hell was Malley doing here at this time of the night? 'What do you want?' he asked nervously.

'I told you. I got to talk to you.'

'So talk.'

'Hey, I'm not talking to you through the door,

Phelps. You want us to wake your neighbours? Open the door.' Malley was beginning to sound angry. Phelps knew he had no choice. If he didn't open it he knew Malley was capable of breaking the cheap lock with one shove.

Reluctantly he unlocked the door. Malley strode into the room, a frown on his face. His wide bulk made the small bedsit seem even smaller.

Phelps shut the door and faced Malley. He noticed he was carrying a small briefcase. 'How'd you find me?'

Malley gave an amused snort and sat down on Phelp's bed, making it creak in protest. 'All it took was a couple of phone calls. You've got a lot to learn about going to ground, kid ...'

'Look, about that bank job ... Simmons told me he'd cleared it with Mr Harris. I didn't know until afterwards that he was operating on his lonesome ...'

Malley held up a beefy hand. 'Settle down, kid. Mr Harris knows the full story. He doesn't blame you. In fact, he's going to help you. He's fixed it for you to get out of the country, this morning. That's why I'm here ...' He tapped the briefcase resting on his lap. 'I've got your tickets. In a few hours you're going to be on your way to Spain.'

'I am?' said Phelps wonderingly, not daring to believe his luck.

'Course, Mr Harris expects payment for his efforts, know what I mean?'

'Yeah.' Phelps nodded warily. 'How much?'

'A cut of the bank proceeds. Twenty per cent.'

'Twenty per cent?!'

Malley said quietly, 'All things considered, I reckon you're getting off light. You want me to tell Mr Harris you don't appreciate his generosity?'

'No — no, of course not. Twenty per cent it is.'

Malley smiled. 'Good lad. So where is the money stashed?'

Phelps pointed at a chest of drawers. 'Right there.'

Malley stared at him. 'You mean you kept it *with* you?'

'Yeah, sure ...' said Phelps. 'Shouldn't I have?'

Malley grimaced. 'Talk about a one hundred per cent amateur. How you managed to stay out of the hands of the Old Bill is a mystery. Well, from now on things are going to be different. You're going to learn how to be a pro. Get the money and your things together — we're getting out of here.'

'Sure, Malley. I'll be ready in just two shakes,' Phelps told him eagerly. He turned and pulled open the drawers. At the same time Malley opened the briefcase and took out a Walther PK automatic fitted with a long silencer. Then he shot Phelps twice in the back of the head.

Dempsey wasn't sure whether it was pounding on the door or the pounding in his head that was the more aggravating. Feeling groggy he rolled out of bed and staggered to the door. When he opened it and saw Detective Chief Inspector Lacey, Detective Sergeant Taylor and a uniformed constable standing in the hallway he knew the day was going to get off to a bad start. 'Hi, guys,' he muttered. 'What's the ...?'

Lacey didn't let him finish the question. With his face set in a stony mask, Lacey said grimly. 'James Dempsey? I am a police officer. I have a warrant to search these premises.' He produced a folded document from inside his overcoat, then pushed past Dempsey into his living room. Taylor and the constable followed wordlessly.

Dempsey, feeling stunned, said, 'Hey, what is this? What the hell game do you think you're playing?'

'The game is a murder investigation,' Lacey told him as he watched his men begin to search the living room. They were none too tidy about it.

Dempsey felt his temper start to flare when Taylor cleared a book shelf by simply sweeping the row of books onto the floor. 'You wanna tell me what's goin' on here?' he growled at Lacey.

Lacey ignored the question. 'Where's your gun, Dempsey?'

'My gun?' Dempsey frowned. 'Why?'

'I asked you where it was?'

'In the bedroom. Top drawer of the bureau. You want me to go get it, *sir*?'

'No.' Lacey turned to the constable. 'Winters, go and fetch the Lieutenant's gun.'

The constable disappeared into the bedroom. Meanwhile Taylor was turning the sofa on its back and was starting to pull away the hessian covering its base.

Dempsey stepped forward. 'Okay, hold it right there!' he warned. Taylor paused, looking at Lacey for direction.

Lacey said to Dempsey, 'Going to be sensible, are we? Going to tell us where you put it?'

'I'll tell you what I'm gonna be,' said Dempsey angrily. 'In about one second I'm gonna be mad as hell and you're gonna be flat on your high-ranking ass.'

'Make sure that goes on the record, Taylor,' said Lacey as he stared contemptuously at Dempsey. 'Lieutenant Dempsey threatened me with the intention of obstructing me in the execution of my duty.'

'Yessir,' said Taylor solemnly.

At that moment the constable returned with Dempsey's Colt Cobra. He was holding it in his gloved hand by the barrel. As Dempsey took note of this he had a sinking feeling in his stomach.

'What's all *that* for?' he asked.

'Standard procedure in the handling of a suspected murder weapon,' Lacey informed him. 'You should know that, Lieutenant.'

'*Murder* weapon?'

'Bert Simmons was found last night with a .45 bullet lodged in his heart,' said Lacey. 'And I have reason to believe the bullet was fired by your gun.'

Dempsey sagged inwardly but kept his concern from showing on his face. He knew now how the mysterious Mr Big had implicated him with Simmons' death. When he'd been unconscious the killer, or killers, had taken his Colt, used it to kill Simmons then replaced it near him. He cursed himself for not thinking of that possibility but it was too late now.

Lacey was scrutinising him. 'Gone awfully quiet all of a sudden, Yank. Unusual for a loudmouth like you.'

'I've been framed,' said Dempsey. 'even *you* should be able to see that.'

'Framed, my arse,' sneered Lacey. To Taylor he said, 'Proceed.'

Taylor ripped away the hessian at the base of the sofa and stuck his hand inside. Then Taylor did something out of character. He grinned.

He withdrew his hand. It was now clutching a fat packet. He handed it to Lacey. Lacey glanced triumphantly at Dempsey then tore open the envelope, revealing a thick wad of bank notes. He waved them under Dempsey's nose. 'What's this. Your nest egg?'

'I've never seen them before,' said Dempsey resign-edly. He knew he was wasting his time.

Lacey put the envelope in his pocket. 'James Dempsey, I am arresting you for the murder of Bert Simmons. I must warn you that anything you say ...'

Dempsey held up a hand. 'Save your breath, Lacey. I know the script.'

Lacey glared at him then said to Taylor, 'Cuff him.'

'You're kidding,' said Dempsey.

'Are you resisting arrest, Dempsey?' There was a glitter in Lacey's eyes. Dempsey knew he was itching for the opportunity to 'restrain' him physically so he decided to play it safe. He offered his wrists and said sarcastically, 'It's okay, sheriff, I'll go quietly.'

Makepeace was still in a mild state of shock. It was all so unbelievable. Dempsey under arrest for murder! And she under interrogation in Spikings' office as if she was under suspicion of being an accomplice. Apart from Spikings and Lacey there was also a police stenographer present and it gave her a very strange feeling to be the one being questioned instead of vice versa ...

'... But you went to Simmons' house with Demp-sey,' Lacey was saying. 'In direct defiance of Chief Superintendent Spiking's orders. Why?'

Wearily, Makepeace answered, 'He had informa-tion.'

'Dempsey tell you that? Say he was going to break in as well, did he?'

'No, he didn't. I've already said what happened. We saw Simmons drive off. It was obviously a spur-of-the-moment decision of Dempsey's ...'

'Obviously,' said Lacey dryly.

Makepeace looked to Spikings for help but he refused to meet her eye. She looked back at Lacey. 'You don't know Dempsey.'

'Oh yes I do. I've come across his type before. A bent cop is a bent cop.'

Makepeace said nothing. Only the flush of her cheeks revealed her rapidly growing anger.

'I suppose you're going to tell me you knew nothing about his rendezvous with Simmons at the Park Palace site last night?'

'No. Nothing at all.'

'You're his partner. I hear you two are very thick ...' He paused and smirked at her. 'Thick as thieves, you might say.'

She narrowed her eyes at him. 'I wouldn't say that. I would say as thick as a Divisional C.I.D ...'

'Makepeace, that'll do,' cut in Spikings hastily. 'For now, at least. Send Dempsey in.'

Dempsey was leaning against the wall in the passageway outside Spikings' office. Detective Sergeant Taylor was nearby.

'They want you,' Makepeace told him, her voice chilly.

'How'd it go in there?' he asked her.

'I may have just blown my career for you.'

He grinned at her. 'Don't sweat it, Makepeace. I'll do the same for you.'

'That's a *big* help,' she said and walked off.

Dempsey watched her go for a few moments then opened the door to Spikings' office and strode in. 'Hi, guys!' he said brightly. 'You come to your senses yet or am I still under arrest?'

'You're still under arrest, cowboy,' said Lacey. 'Sit down.'

Dempsey sat down in the straight-backed chair in front of Spikings' desk. Lacey prowled about the office like a restless animal.

Dempsey looked around with mock surprise. 'You call this a Third Degree. Where are the bright lights? The truncheons?'

'This is no laughing matter, Dempsey,' Lacey told him grimly. 'A murder charge is serious business.'

'Gee whiz, really? All my years as a cop and no one ever told me that before.'

Spikings said, 'You're not helping yourself, Lieutenant Dempsey.'

Dempsey shrugged. 'Okay, I confess. Sure I took the money. It was in Simmons' kitchen — in a cookie jar marked "Swag". I dunno how you guys missed it.'

'Come on, I want the facts,' said Lacey impatiently. 'You broke into Simmons' house, you found part of the proceeds from the bank robbery. Then you got greedy. You told Simmons to meet you. You said you wanted more. He refused so you shot him and then dumped his body in the cement. You were in the process of covering him up when you were disturbed by the arrival of a patrol car. Right?'

Dempsey nodded. 'Yeah, I iced him okay. Call it cementing Anglo-American relations.'

A dark red flush began to move up Lacey's neck. 'Think you're being clever, eh, cowboy?'

Angrily, Dempsey said, 'I think I'm being hung out to dry is what I think! I'm being framed, you idiot. I'm being framed every which way! Right now I wouldn't look out of place hanging in the Tate Gallery, you dumb cop!'

'Dempsey . . .' began Spikings warningly.

'Hey no!' said Dempsey, turning to him. 'Hear me out, Chief! Am I some kind of goddamn amateur? Would I leave my prints all over the scene of a robbery? Would I hide the money in my sofa?! Would I murder a guy with my *own* gun?! No way! It's a set up and you know it.'

'But the evidence against you, Dempsey, is pretty strong,' said Spikings non-committally.

'Chief, Simmons didn't have any money at his home. I don't think he had any of the bank's money at all. If he did it would have had to come from his wheel man. And why would this guy give Simmons a cut from his own share after Simmons had fouled up so badly at the bank? No, you want some answers you find that wheel man.'

'We did,' said Lacey.

'Yeah?' said Dempsey, surprised. He looked expectantly at Lacey. 'So what did he say?'

'Not a lot. No brains. Someone had put two bullets in the back of his head.'

Dempsey digested this information then said, 'That someone supposed to be me?'

' *Was* it you?'

Dempsey simply laughed.

'The bullets were 9mm, not .45s,' said Spikings.

Lacey frowned at him. 'So Dempsey has two guns.'

'Tell me something,' said Dempsey. 'How do you know this stiff was Simmons' wheel man?'

Lacey hesitated before answering. Then he said, 'Tip-off.'

'Uh-huh,' nodded Dempsey. 'And I suppose you got a tip-off that some of the bank money could be found at my place. Aren't you kind of curious about who is being so helpful to you?'

Lacey shrugged. 'A criminal associate of Simmons'

61

who wants to get even with you, no doubt. I don't think that matters too much . . .'

'Well, *I* sure do, buddy,' Dempsey told him angrily.

'Cowboy, you can twist and turn as much as you like but it's not going to change the fact that you've been well and truly hooked,' said Lacey. 'So why not do us all a favour and come clean.'

Dempsey stood up and faced him. 'Lacey,' he said, his voice low and menacing, 'I've met some dumb cops in my time but you're the dumbest. Just because you've got some chip on your shoulder about me you're refusing to face the truth. In my book that's about as stupid as a cop can get.'

'That's enough,' snapped Spikings before Lacey could reply. Then, 'I'd like five minutes alone with the Lieutenant if that's all right with you.'

'I wouldn't mind five minutes alone with him myself,' said Lacey, glowering at Dempsey.

Dempsey said, 'No you wouldn't, pal.'

'Five minutes,' Lacey told Spikings. 'Then he's mine.'

'You haven't got the authorisation yet,' said Spikings.

'But I soon will have,' said Lacey, going to the door. 'Five minutes, that's all.'

When Lacey had gone, Spikings looked at Dempsey and said, 'You're a clown, Dempsey.'

'Yeah. But under the greasepaint my heart is breaking.'

'Shut up! You are in trouble. Big trouble. Big like Texas is big.'

Dempsey's shoulders sagged slightly. In a different tone of voice he said, 'I know it, Chief.'

'Then stop acting like Dirty Harry and start trying to help yourself. Right now Detective Chief Inspector

Lacey is out there calling his Divisional Commander for authorisation to take you back to Holborn and keep you there. I had to pull strings to make Lacey bring you here, and what do you do — make him angry!'

'He was already angry with me. The guy hates my guts. I dunno why. Maybe his mother had a bad experience with an American G.I. during the war. Maybe he still resents the fact that Britain lost the American colonies. How should I know? All I know is that he wants to nail my ass to the wall.'

'And he's going to do it,' Spikings grimly. 'No way round that. Even on circumstantial evidence alone he's got you. You're facing fifteen years, Dempsey, to put it bluntly.'

'Hey, come on, Chief! You don't believe any of this crap, do you? You know me better than that. And you know as well as I do that someone set me up!'

'What I believe doesn't matter. It's out of my hands.' He sighed. 'I warned you, didn't I? Stay away from Simmons case, I said, but no, you had to play the lone ranger. And look where it's got you.' He shook his head sadly.

'Chief, *why* did you tell me to lay off the case?' Dempsey asked.

Spikings looked at him. 'I was ordered to. By Lacey's Divisional Commander.'

'Didn't that seem fishy to you?'

'No. Lacey had made a complaint about you which was perfectly justified. You were meddling in a case that was out of your jurisdiction.'

'Well, it still seems fishy to me,' muttered Dempsey.

Spikings was silent for a time then stood up. 'I'm going to get a cup of tea. You'd better be here when I get back. Because if you do a bunk I won't be able to help you. Do you understand what I'm saying, Lieutenant?'

'Loud and clear, Chief,' said Dempsey, and grinned.

Chapter
SEVEN

Makepeace was feeling terrible as she parked her car in the basement carpark of her block of flats. It had been quite the worst day of her life. First Dempsey's arrest, then her being suspected of being his accomplice and then, to top it off, his escape from S.I.10 headquarters and subsequent disappearance.

She was definitely not in the mood for entertaining tonight but unfortunately she had already invited Nigel around again in an attempt to make up for the débâcle of the previous night . . .

She was just getting the groceries out of the back of the car when she heard a sound behind her. She whirled round, hand reaching for her .32 inside her jacket. There was a figure standing in the shadows by the wall. A man . . .

'Who's there?' she called sharply.

The figure stepped out of the shadows.

'Oh, hell,' she sighed. It was Dempsey.

'You don't seem pleased to see me, princess,' he said.

'How very perceptive of you.'

'Aren't you going to invite me in?'

'No.'

'Hey, come on, be a pal. I haven't stopped moving all afternoon. I'm starving. At least let me have a sandwich.'

'Dempsey, I am already in enough trouble thanks to you. I don't want to look back one day and reflect on the fact that I lost my career over a cheese sandwich.'

'So make it a ham, tomato, lettuce and coleslaw sandwich. On rye bread, if you got any.'

'I don't have any rye bread.'

'It's okay, I'm easy. I'll take white.'

She sighed. 'Oh, very well. Come up then ... but not for long.'

Ten minutes later Dempsey was seated on her living room sofa and eagerly devouring a huge sandwich that she had made under his detailed instructions. 'You need a shave,' she informed him coldly.

'I know,' he agreed around a mouthful of ham, tomato, lettuce and coleslaw. 'But I didn't have time this morning. Being arrested and all kind of interfered with my usual routine.'

'How's your head?'

'My "self-inflicted injury" as Lacey put it? Hurts like hell.'

'I'll fetch you some aspirin.' She went back into the kitchen and returned with two aspirin and a glass of water. She set them down on the coffee table in front of him, then stood there regarding him with a severe expression. 'You made a lot of assumptions coming here. You know that, don't you?'

'Where else could I go, princess? You're the only real friend I've got in this town.'

'I'd be flattered, Dempsey, if it wasn't for the fact that you're a fugitive and I'm a police officer and there's a warrant out for your arrest. For murder. In other words, what we have here is a conflict of interests. You have put me in a very awkward situation ...'

'How come?' he said, finishing the remains of the sandwich.

'Ever hear of a little thing called Duty, Dempsey?'

He nodded. 'Yeah. I've heard of that. Comes somewhere under Loyalty. You heard of Loyalty, princess?'

'Yes, I've heard of Loyalty, Lieutenant. But what I'd also like to hear is one good reason why I shouldn't arrest you and turn you in right now. That's the question Lacey is going to ask me after *I'm* arrested as an accessory.'

'Because you know I'm innocent.'

'Yes, I *know* you're innocent but what I'd like is some *evidence.*'

'So would I,' he said with feeling. 'So would I.'

She sighed. 'I'm going to have a shower. A long, hot one. Help yourself to a drink. And try and think of a way out of this mess while I'm gone ...'

Makepeace made the spray of water as hot as she could stand it. She always found a very hot shower a good remedy for fatigue and shattered nerves. And she was suffering from an excess of both at the moment ...

She gave a start of alarm when she saw the bathroom door suddenly open. Then Dempsey stuck his head round it and her alarm turned to livid indignation.

'Dempsey! What the hell do you think you're doing!!?' she cried as she tried to conceal herself with the shower curtain.

He put his fingers to his lips and gestured that she should turn off the taps. She did so. 'What the . . .?'

'Shush,' he told her quietly. 'The doorbell just rang. Are you expecting company?'

'No, of course n . . .' Then she remembered Nigel. 'Oh God, yes, I am! It's probably Nigel. I forgot all about him, thanks to you.'

'If it is him go tell him to get lost.'

'I will *not*,' she said indignantly. 'And will you please get *out* of my bathroom!'

He obediently withdrew his head. Makepeace hurriedly wrapped a towel around herself. With the shower turned off she could now hear the doorbell herself. She ran past Dempsey. 'Stay out of sight,' she hissed. 'In case it's *not* Nigel.'

She opened the door. It was Nigel. For a moment he looked surprised at the state she was in, then a slow, lascivious smile spread across his face. 'Why, Harriet, darling, how nice! You should greet me like this more often.'

Makepeace pulled the towel, which was already slipping, up higher. 'Sorry about this, Nigel, but I'm rather behind schedule. Come in . . .'

His smile widened as he entered. 'Nothing to be sorry about, darling. On the contrary, you look delightful. You should get behind schedule more often . . .' He took hold of her bare shoulders and kissed her. Makepeace pulled back.

'Nigel, please, not now. There's something I have to . . .'

'Why Harriet,' he said, with amusement. 'You're all flustered. I don't think I've ever seen you this way before, You're always so cool, calm and collected.'

'I'm not flustered,' she said, irritably. 'It's just that ... that ...' He didn't allow her to finish. He kissed her again and then said, 'Let's finish the conversation in your bedroom. We can eat later ...' She felt his hands fumbling with the knot of the towel behind her back. 'Nigel, don't ...' She pulled away from him but he followed, his smile growing more lascivious by the second.

Then, abruptly, the smile vanished. 'What the ...?' he said in astonishment, staring over her shoulder She turned, knowing with a sinking heart what she was going to see ...

And there, as expected, was Dempsey, leaning against the kitchen doorway with a huge grin on his face. 'Hey, don't mind me, you guys. Finish what you started. I'm broad-minded.'

'Dempsey, you ...'

'Harriet, what's *he* doing here?' demanded Nigel, his voice quivering with anger.

She sighed. 'It's a long story.'

'Actually, pal, I just popped in for a sandwich.'

Nigel looked at him and then at Makepeace. The towel was starting to sag again. A sick realization appeared in Nigel Penward's eyes. 'Harriet, you haven't ... not with *him*?'

'What?' she said, not understanding what he meant for a few seconds. Then, as awareness sank in, she said indignantly, 'No, of course not, Nigel! It's not how it looks!'

'Then what's he doing here, Harriet? I mean to say, this is the second night in a row he's turned up.'

'I told you, pal,' said Dempsey. 'I dropped in for a bite to eat.'

Makepeace took a deep breath — a precarious manoeuvre in her towel — and said, 'Dempsey's on the run. He's wanted for murder.'

Penward blinked stupidly at her. 'I beg your pardon?'

Dempsey threw up his hands in disgust. 'That's right, tell the whole world.'

'The whole world already knows, Dempsey!' she cried. 'There's an APB out on you. You were on the *news* ...' She turned to Penward. 'You must have heard about it.'

He frowned. 'Well, yes. I did hear a mention on the car radio of some London detective being sought in connection with a murder enquiry but I wasn't paying much attention ... I didn't know it referred to *him*.' He pointed to Dempsey.

'Well, it does,' said Makepeace. 'And that's why he's here. It's all perfectly innocent.'

'Innocent?' cried Penward. 'But he's an escaped murderer!'

'I meant ... Oh, never mind. Look, Nigel, Dempsey is no murderer. He's been framed.'

'She's telling the truth, pal,' said Dempsey.

Penward regarded him dubiously. 'Well, you *would* say that, wouldn't you?'

'Yeah. I would.'

'Can you prove it?'

'Ah, that's where we get into some tricky territory.'

Penward turned back to Makepeace. 'Harriet, be reasonable about this. You can't afford to be mixed up with him, whether he's guilty or not. You've got your reputation to think of. How would your father, Lord Winfield, feel if it was spread all over the papers

70

that his policewoman daughter had been aiding and abetting an escaped felon? The disgrace would kill him.'

'Don't you think I haven't thought about that?' said Makepeace unhappily.

'"An escaped felon",' muttered Dempsey. 'I'll remember that one, pal.'

'And if you won't think about your father, think about us,' continued Penward. 'A scandal like that would mean our marriage was out of the question . . .'

'Well, at least some good will come out of all this, princess,' said Dempsey.

'Oh shut up! I'm trying to think . . .'

The door bell rang again. Dempsey looked at Makepeace. 'One guess who that is,' he said quietly.

A fist began to pound on the door. 'Lacey,' said Makepeace.

'Well, princess, what now? I'm in your hands,' said Dempsey, still looking at her.

She made up her mind. 'Back in the bathroom, quick!' she told him. Then she said quickly to Penward, 'It's probably the police. Led by a man called Lacey. Tell him I'm taking a shower. And if he asks you about Dempsey, you haven't seen him, right?'

Penward gaped at her in disbelief. 'You're asking *me* to become an accessory now?!'

'One little lie, that's all. If you love me you'll do it, otherwise . . .' She left the threat hanging in the air as she hurried after Dempsey.

Penward stood there in the living room for several long moments listening to the pounding on the front door which had increased in volume. Then, after taking a deep breath, he went and opened it.

Lacey stared at him and said, 'Who the hell are you?'

'I could say the same about you,' said Penward, taking an immediate dislike to him.

'I'm Detective Chief Inspector Lacey and I have a warrant to search these premises,' said Lacey and made a move to enter but Penward held up a restraining hand.

'Just a moment. My name is Nigel Penward — the *Honourable* Nigel Penward — and I'd like to see that warrant.'

Lacey glared at him but then, with ill grace, produced the warrant. 'Where's Sergeant Makepeace?' he snapped as Penward examined the document.

'Taking a shower, actually.' He handed the warrant back. 'It seems to be in order. You and your men may come in.'

'Thank *you*, sir,' said Lacey with heavy sarcasm. He and Detective Sergeant Taylor entered, followed by two uniformed constables. 'Right,' Lacey told them. 'Search the place thoroughly. And I *do* mean thoroughly.'

As the three officers disappeared into the other rooms Lacey looked Penward up and down and said, 'What's your business here tonight, sir?'

Penward went to the drinks cabinet and poured himself a gin and tonic. He didn't offer Lacey a drink. Finally he drawled, 'My *business* here is purely social. Miss Makepeace happens to be my fiancée.'

'Oh,' said Lacey, momentarily caught off-guard. Then he said, 'Are you two alone here tonight?'

Penward raised an eyebrow. 'I don't follow you.'

'It was a perfectly straightforward question, sir. Is there anyone else in this flat apart from you and Sergeant Makepeace?'

'Not to my knowledge, Detective Sergeant,'

answered Penward blandly. 'Why do you ask?'

'It's Detective *Chief Inspector*. And the reason I ask is that we're searching for a colleague of your fiancée's — an American by the name of Dempsey.'

'I know the one you mean,' nodded Penward. 'Met him once. Boorish fellow. No manners.'

'That's the one. Have you seen him?'

'Yes, I have actually ...'

'Tonight?!' asked Lacey eagerly.

Penward frowned. 'No. Last night.'

'Oh.' Lacey's disappointment was palpable. 'Look, would you mind fetching Sergeant Makepeace — your fiancée — out of the shower? I want to talk to her.'

Penward's response was to give a shrug, then go and sit down in an armchair. 'It's your show, Detective Chief Inspector, so why don't you go and fetch her? I'm sure she'll be delighted to see you.'

Lacey frowned at him. Upper class twit, he thought. Mocking me ... Lacey turned on his heel and marched off towards the bathroom. On the way he encountered Taylor. 'Not a sign of him, sir. But there's someone in the bathroom.'

'I know,' said Lacey grimly. He stopped at the bathroom door and raised his hand to knock on it. Then he hesitated. It occurred to him that Sergeant Makepeace was taking an inordinately long time with her shower. Either she liked long showers or ...

'Cover me, Taylor,' he whispered.

Taylor looked puzzled but obediently drew his .32 revolver just the same.

Lacey slowly turned the door handle then flung the door open with a crash ...

Chapter
EIGHT

Lacey had more than half-convinced himself that he
was going to see Dempsey hiding in the bathroom and
so was taken by surprise when all he saw was Makepeace standing naked in her bath under the shower.

His initial reaction, apart from disappointment at
not finding Dempsey, was to be struck by the realization that Sergeant Makepeace was an unusually
attractive woman. Her reaction, on the other hand,
was to scream and make a grab for the edge of the
shower curtain. Then, when she recognized Lacey,
her shocked expression turned to one of livid anger.
'What the hell do you think you're doing?!' she cried
as she pulled the curtain closed.

Lacey was now feeling acutely embarrassed. Never
usually at a loss for words, he found he couldn't think
of a thing to say. 'Er ... er ...' he stammered, then
began to back out of the doorway, bumping into
Taylor who was also gazing at Makepeace in awe-

struck wonder. Recovering the power of speech, Lacey took out his embarrassment on Taylor. 'Don't just stand there, you fool! And put that gun away ...' He gave Taylor a shove and slammed the door behind him.

'They've gone,' Makepeace whispered hoarsely to Dempsey who was lying face down in the bath between her feet. 'Don't move until I tell you ...'

'It's okay, princess,' he said, his voice muffled. 'I can't see a thing. But you'd better hurry before I drown down here ...'

He heard Makepeace get out of the bath and then, a short time later, she said, 'All right, you can get up now.'

Dempsey, soaking wet, raised himself from the bottom of the bath. He saw that Makepeace was hurriedly wrapping herself in towels. He grinned at her. 'Well, it worked.'

She looked furious. 'The things I do for you! I still don't see why I had to leave the shower curtain open. I've never been so *embarrassed*.'

'Because if you hadn't Lacey would have remembered once he'd recovered his wits and come back to check it out.'

'Hmph!' said Makepeace, not sounding convinced.

Dempsey got behind the curtain. 'Now do your best to get rid of them as soon as you can.'

'You don't need to tell *me* that!' she hissed and opened the door.

Makepeace didn't have to feign anger as she came out of the bathroom and into the living room — she *was* angry. At Lacey, at Dempsey, at herself and at the whole goddamn mess.

'Detective Chief Inspector Lacey, have you ever heard of *knocking* before you barge into a lady's bathroom?!' she demanded as she bore down on him.

His face red he backed away from her until he came in contact with the wall and could go no further. 'My apologies ... Sergeant Makepeace,' he stammered. 'But I had reason to believe that you were harbouring a fugitive from justice in ... in ...'

'In my bathroom?' she said icily.

'Er, well ... yes.'

She glanced at Nigel. 'You've met my boyfriend here?'

'Er, yes ... He said he was your fiancé.'

'So you take me to be the sort of woman who goes and takes a shower with another man while my fiancé sits calmly out here?'

Lacey went a deeper shade of red. 'Er ...'

One of the uniformed officers sniggered. Lacey shot him a poisonous look that silenced him instantly.

'Well?' said Makepeace.

Lacey pulled himself to his full height. 'I can only say again that I'm sorry, Sergeant Makepeace.'

'I should think so.'

'Then I take it you haven't seen Lieutenant Dempsey since he absconded from S.I.10 this afternoon?'

'No, I haven't.'

'You will, of course, notify either me or Spikings if he does make contact with you?'

Makepeace fixed him with a cold stare. 'Are you now suggesting I wouldn't fulfill my duty as a police officer?' she asked.

'Er, no ... no ... nothing like that. It's just that ...' At that point he gave up. 'All right, all right, we're going now. Come on, men ...'

He quickly ushered Taylor and the other two officers out of the flat. At the front door he paused and looked back at Makepeace. 'I'll speak to you again tomorrow, Sergeant. In Spikings' office. First thing tomorrow morning.'

She nodded. 'Very well. Good night, Detective Chief Inspector.'

He grunted something and shut the door.

Makepeace gave a deep sigh and went and collapsed on the sofa beside Penward. He was regarding her with an expression somewhere between wonder and surprise. 'I must say this evening has been quite a revelation, Harriet. I've seen sides of you I never suspected existed.'

'*Everyone's* been seeing too many of my sides tonight,' she muttered angrily. 'Join the club.'

Just then Dempsey, still dripping water, entered the living room. 'I caught some of your performance, princess. You should have been an actress.'

'When I get thrown off the police force — which will probably happen tomorrow — I'll go try RADA. And don't drip on my carpet.'

Penward said to Dempsey, 'Well, now that we've saved your bacon you can get going. I'd say it's been a pleasure meeting you again but it hasn't.'

'Hey, where do you expect me to go like this?' asked Dempsey.

'Try an aquarium.'

'Wise guy.'

'Stop bickering, you two. Dempsey, go back into the bathroom and get out of those wet things. I'll fetch you something to put on while I dry your clothes.'

'Thanks, princess.' He headed back to the bathroom.

'And *then* he goes, right?' said Penward.

Makepeace shook her head reluctantly. 'Nigel, be reasonable, he hasn't got anyplace *to* go. I'm going to have to let him stay here until morning.'

'You're not serious!'

'It's the safest place for him to be at the moment. Lacey won't be back — not tonight anyway.'

'But you're digging yourself deeper and deeper into this situation, Harriet. Be reasonable!'

'Nigel,' she sighed, 'I *have* to help him. He's my partner. There's such a thing as loyalty.'

'There's such a thing as professional suicide too. You can't throw away your career on this American boor.'

'Not long ago you were asking me to give up my career for you, Nigel.'

'But that's different.'

She didn't answer.

'Well, isn't it?' he demanded.

'Don't press me, Nigel. I'm very tired.' She got up. 'I'm going to put on some clothes ...'

'Harriet, answer me!'

But she hurried out of the room.

When Dempsey returned wrapped in a blanket he found Makepeace, dressed in jeans and blouse, sitting alone on the sofa and sipping a large scotch. There was no sign of Penward.

'Where's lover boy?'

'Gone,' said Makepeace, not looking at him. 'Help yourself to a drink. You must need one. I know I do.'

He did so then sat down opposite her. 'Pissed off, was he?'

'Yes. Wouldn't you be in his position?'

Dempsey shrugged but decided not to pursue the subject. 'Hey, princess, I really appreciate what you did tonight. I won't forget it.'

'Nor will I.'

'I'll do the same for you one day.'

'I hope not.' She took another sip of her drink and continued to stare moodily into space.

'Uh, princess,' he said hesitantly. 'There's one more favour I'd like to ask . . .'

'Sure, you can stay tonight. But *just* for tonight.'

'Hey,' he said, surprised. 'You're an angel, princess!'

'I'm an idiot.'

After an uncomfortable silence Dempsey said, 'Uh, actually there's just *one* more favour I want from you.'

'The answer is no. You sleep here on the sofa.'

He looked puzzled for a moment then laughed. 'No, not *that.* I need some money. I haven't got my cheque book and I'm almost out of cash.'

'I've only got about ten pounds in my purse,' she told him. 'I'll give it to you in the morning.'

'Thanks, but I'm gonna need more than that. No telling how long I'm gonna have to lay low.'

'How much more?'

'How's three hundred quid sound?'

'Too bloody much.'

'I'll pay you back.'

'Huh!'

'Please, princess. It's survival money.'

She sighed. 'I'll go to the bank tomorrow morning and meet you somewhere at lunchtime.'

He patted her on the shoulder. 'Thanks, princess.'

She looked at him. 'You know, I'd save myself a lot of trouble if I simply turned you in.'

'But you wouldn't, would you?'

'Don't tempt me, Dempsey. Just don't tempt me.'

Lacey had recovered his dignity by the following morning and was every inch the unbending Detective Chief Inspector as he sat behind Spikings' desk and grimly surveyed Makepeace who stood stiffly before him. She felt like a schoolgirl who had been summoned to the headmaster's office.

'I'll keep this short, Sergeant. I'm going to ask you again, for the record, if you have any knowledge of the present whereabouts of James Dempsey?'

'No sir, I don't.' This wasn't a lie as she didn't know where he was at the moment. He had been at her flat that morning and at 12.30 he was going to be at the Three Greyhounds pub in Old Compton Street but right now she didn't have a clue as to his whereabouts.

'Do you want to reconsider that answer, Sergeant? This is your last chance.'

'No sir. Can I go now, sir?'

Lacey's eyes were like two gun barrels. 'When I'm finished, Sergeant . . .'

Makepeace waited, trying to conceal her nervousness.

'Sergeant, I'll tell you bluntly, I don't believe you. I think you're helping your transatlantic friend. So the next time you run across him give him a message from me — tell him he may have made a fool of the law but no chance is he going to make a fool of *me*. Better men than he have tried and failed. You tell him that, Sergeant.'

'I think you'd do better by putting an announcement in *The Times*, sir.'

'Don't be facetious, Sergeant!' he snapped.

'Sorry, sir, But let me ask you something — do you really believe those stupid charges against Lieutenant Dempsey?'

'What I believe, in my soul, I tell God. And when I'm wrong God let's me know. He's given me no indication that I am wrong on this occasion. So I am going to get Dempsey. And I'm going to get anybody that helps him. Understand?'

'Perfectly, sir.'

'You're under arrest,' said a voice quietly into Dempsey's left ear.

He turned and grinned. 'Hi, princess. You're late.'

Makepeace hoisted herself onto the barstool beside him. 'Big queue at the bank.' She opened her purse and took out a small bundle of ten pound notes. She put them on the bar. 'There you are, three hundred pounds. And now I'm overdrawn, for the first time in ages. I *hate* being overdrawn.'

'I told you I'd pay you back.'

'Dempsey, since yesterday I've blown my career, I've conspired to pervert the course of justice, I've jeopardized my relationship with Nigel and for the first time in six years I'm overdrawn at the bank. You will never — if you live to be three hundred years old — be able to pay me back.'

He picked up the money and put it in his inside jacket pocket. 'One day you'll thank me.'

'Come again?'

'For screwing up your romance with Lord Fauntleroy. He's not for you, princess. The guy's a jerk. It would never work out if you married him.'

'Shut up, Dempsey, and buy me a drink. A double vodka.'

Dempsey summoned over Peter, the publican of the Three Greyhounds, and ordered Makepeace's drink, as well as another scotch and soda for himself. 'Did you bring the info on Simmons I wanted?' he asked her.

'Yes, but it wasn't easy getting it out of the computer. Spikings was on my back all morning. Wants results on the Holdstock case. And we're still looking for leads on that Arab Prince kidnapping ...' She opened her shoulder bag and produced a computer print-out. Dempsey took it and started to scan quickly through it.

As he read he rubbed his chin thoughtfully. The gesture made a rasping sound. 'You *really* need a shave now,' she told him. 'You're beginning to look very untidy. Your suit needs pressing too.'

'If I'd found a razor at your place I would have shaved this morning before I left. I looked everywhere but you must have a great hiding place for it.'

'I don't own a razor, Dempsey. I don't need one.'

He looked up from the print-out. 'Yeah?' he said.

'Yeah.'

'You know, you must be the first dame I've come across who doesn't have to shave her legs.'

'How fascinating, Dempsey,' she said dryly. 'I'll be sure to jot that down in my diary tonight.'

He returned his attention to the print-out. 'You do that.'

'So what do you think?' she asked.

'About your legs?'

'About the stuff on Simmons,' she said irritably.

'Interesting,' he admitted. 'We now know he used to work for Harris-Strang but where does that take us?'

She pointed towards the bottom of the sheet. 'See?

They're clients of Endicott, Drake and Armitage.'

'Hmmm,' he said. 'I get the feeling we're beginning to see a pattern here.' He read further. 'Simmons was site foreman, then quarry manager. What would he make on that job?'

'Probably about fifteen thousand a year.'

'I've seen his bankbook. He was making a hell of a lot more than that. At least he was before he went into business for himself.'

'So he was on the fiddle when he was working for Harris-Strang. He had latent criminal tendencies, remember? Like a lot of people. They start off breaking into people's houses and the next thing you know they're wanted for murder.'

Dempsey ignored the jibe. He made the rasping sound on his chin again and mused, 'He could have been ripping Harris off to set up his own business. Three years ago. But why's it surfaced now? Harris-Strang — that name keeps ringing bells.'

'Their men were repairing the bank vault, remember?'

He snapped his fingers. 'The Park Palace Hotel site! I saw their name on the fence!'

Makepeace looked smug. 'There's something else. I made a phone call after I got that print-out and ...' She paused, savouring her moment of triumph.

'Well, go on, princess. Spit it out!'

'That bank, the Frith and Hanway. Harris-Strang didn't just repair it, they also *built* it.'

Chapter
NINE

The Harris-Strang building was a black glass and steel cube on the Euston Road near Warren Street tube station. Makepeace entered the reception area first, followed a short time later by Dempsey. While she went up to one of the two receptionists, who were sitting behind a desk that consisted of a slab of glass mounted on chrome tree trunks, Dempsey hung back and pretended to be interested in a wall-mounted fire extinguisher.

Makepeace showed her I.D. to the receptionist. 'I'd like to speak to the manager, please. It's urgent.'

The receptionist, a harassed-looking girl in her early twenties, frowned at the I.D., frowned at Makepeace then glanced worriedly at Dempsey. Then she picked up a phone, punched a number and said, with an East End accent, 'Mr Embrey? There's a police officer to see you. A Sergeant Makepeace . . .'

'I wanted to see Mr Harris,' Makepeace cut in.

The girl put her hand over the mouthpiece. 'Mr Embrey is the manager ...' Then she took her hand away and said, 'Yes sir.' She said to Makepeace, 'Mr Embrey would like to know the reason for your visit.'

'I'm afraid that's between Mr Harris and myself,' said Makepeace stiffly.

The girl repeated this into the phone, said 'Yes sir,' and hung up. She stood. 'Mr Embrey would like to speak to you first. He handles all of Mr Harris's affairs. Would you follow me, please.'

After a helpless glance at Dempsey, Makepeace had no choice but to follow the girl ...

Dempsey quickly came to a decision. He lifted the fire extinguisher off the wall and, ignoring the protests of the other receptionist, ran off with it down a different corridor to the one that Makepeace had entered.

At the first open door he came to he charged through and cried, 'Harris's office! Quick!'

A Eurasian girl of startling beauty stared at him with wide eyes. Wordlessly, she pointed along the corridor. Dempsey ran on. He repeated the routine with a male employee he encountered at a junction of the corridor. 'Embrey said Harris's office! Where's that?' he cried, flourishing the fire extinguisher in a dramatic fashion.

The man pointed at a door a short way along the corridor. Dempsey dashed towards it. He flung it open and found himself in a large outer office. A secretary with the demeanour of a glacier looked at him with a totally unfazed expression and said, 'Yes, can I help you?'

'Don't panic, darling. Dempsey's here ...' he told her as he headed for the double doors leading into the inner office.

'Wait!' she said sternly, 'You can't . . .'

But he was already sliding them apart, and by the time she had got out of her seat he was closing them behind him. The inner office was enormous and dominated by one wall made entirely of glass which gave a spectacular view over London. In front of the glass wall was a large desk — bare except for two phones and a computer terminal — at which was seated an equally large man. He looked enquiringly at Dempsey but didn't seem to be particularly surprised by his unexpected entrance.

Dempsey put the fire extinguisher down and crossed the expanse of thick grey carpet, his hand extended. 'Mr Terence Harris? My name is Lieutenant Dempsey. Glad you could see me . . .'

Harris rose up from his chair and shook Dempsey's hand. 'Hello, Lieutenant Dempsey,' he said blandly.

Dempsey heard the doors open behind him. He turned. The human glacier was there, frowning. 'I'm sorry, Mr Harris, but he just barged by me . . .'

'It's all right, Miss Streatham. Lieutenant Dempsey won't be taking up much of my time, I'm sure. Will you, Lieutenant?'

'No, I just want to ask you a few questions.'

Harris looked at his watch. 'I'm late for a meeting. You can have a couple of minutes. Miss Streatham, would you mind telling the others I'm going to be a little late?'

'I understand, Mr Harris,' she said, and closed the doors.

Harris sat down again. 'Now what do you want to talk to me about, Lieutenant?'

'Bert Simmons. Also late . . .'

* * *

Outside, the glacial Miss Streatham was dialling a number. She waited awhile then said, 'I'd like to speak to Divisional Commander Hopkins, please ...'

'I've already gone through all this with a colleague of yours — Lacey, I think his name was,' said Harris calmly.

'Good old Lacey,' said Dempsey. 'One of my best buddies on the Force. But just for the record I'm afraid I'm going to have to ask you to go through it all again.'

Harris sighed. 'Very well. As I told Lacey I've known Simmons for several years. Since 1981, in fact, when he joined my company. I'd just bought the West London quarry and we put him in as Dispatcher. I'd say he was competent, reliable, well-liked. Embrey, my manager, could probably give you more details about him ...'

'I'm interested in *your* impressions, Mr Harris. Reliable guys don't rob banks.'

'Agreed. It surprised me. But I was aware that he was having business troubles.'

'He started up his lumber yard, what, three years ago?'

Harris nodded. 'Yes, I think that's right.'

'But he still continued to do work for you as well?'

'Yes. As a sub-contractor occasionally.'

'Didn't you ever wonder where he got the money from to start up his own business?'

Harris pursed his lips. 'Not really. I just presumed he had assets of his own. Why? What are you suggesting?'

'I think there was some kind of scam going on here that Simmons was a part of,' said Dempsey.

'*Scam?*'

'Yeah. Maybe they were ripping off construction materials, selling blueprints for high security installations — banks, diamond houses or whatever. You build a lot of those sort of things?'

Harris shook his head. 'No. Only a couple of banks. Mostly hospitals, office blocks, hotels, schools . . . the odd bridge.'

'Well, whatever it was someone was paying him to keep his mouth shut — enough to start up his own business. That went down the tubes so he needed more money — a whole lot more. So he cashed in on what he knew. It put him inside a bank.'

'An interesting theory, Lieutenant,' said Harris, his bland, moon-like face giving nothing away. 'However I can't accept it. This is a very big company but it's still a one-man operation. And I'm that man. I know what goes on in every part of it. I keep track of every nut and bolt so take my word that if there was a "scam" going on I'd know about it.'

'So *is* there a scam going on, Mr Harris?'

For a second Harris's air of bland serenity disappeared and Dempsey got a brief glimpse of the carnivore that lurked behind the carefully maintained camouflage, but then the mask was back in place again and Harris said easily, 'Are you insinuating something, Lieutenant?'

'Me?' asked Dempsey, feigning innocence. 'No sir. I never insinuate anything.'

Harris looked at his watch. 'I'm afraid your time is up. Goodbye, Lieutenant. It was nice talking to you.' He then picked up one of the phones. 'Miss Streatham, Lieutenant Dempsey is leaving now.'

'Okay,' said Dempsey. 'But we'll talk again some other time. Some other time real soon.'

'I doubt that, Lieutenant. Goodbye.'

Dempsey went to the double doors and slid them open. And saw three, grey-suited security men facing him in the outer office.

'Your escort, Lieutenant,' said Harris. 'They will keep you company until your close colleague, Detective Chief Inspector Lacey arrives to collect you, which should be very soon now.'

Dempsey acted. He turned and snatched up the fire extinguisher he'd brought into Harris's office. As the three security men started to rush him he squeezed hard on the extinguisher's release handle and immediately there was a jet of white foam from the nozzle. Dempsey sprayed the three men in their faces, temporarily blinding them, then charged. They went down in a tangle of flailing limbs, cursing and yelling. Dempsey, still spraying foam around, nimbly stepped over them and into the outer office. The glacial secretary, mouth gaping open in shock, was frantically punching numbers on her phone. Dempsey grinned at her. 'Don't think I'm going to leave you out, baby,' he said and aimed the nozzle at her.

The jet of foam hit her directly in the face. She gave a shriek and fell backwards off her chair. Dempsey dropped the extinguisher and hurried into the corridor. He knew he wouldn't have long before Harris had the building sealed off with his security men. He needed a diversion . . .

He saw a fire alarm on the wall ahead. He didn't hesitate. He broke the glass with his elbow then pressed the black button. Instantly the air was filled with the jarring clamour from numerous fire bells. Office doors flew open and people emerged looking surprised and puzzled.

'Is it a drill of what?' asked a woman nearby.

'No, it's the real thing!' cried Dempsey loudly. 'Come on everybody! Get moving! Fast! To the fire exits!'

Very soon a mass exodus was underway towards the nearest fire escape and Dempsey joined in the flow. A short time later he was out on the street. He hurried round to the front of the building where Makepeace's car was parked. She was already there. 'Don't tell me you had something to do with all this,' she said accusingly, nodding towards the crowd of anxious-looking Harris-Strang employees milling about the front entrance.

'I don't know what you mean, princess,' he told her. Then he cocked his ear and said, 'Uh oh ...'

Mixed in with the sirens of the approaching fire engines was the unmistakable sound of a police car klaxon. 'Quick, gimme your car keys!'

She gave them to him with a frown. 'What ...?' she began. But Dempsey was already leaping into her car. 'Will call you later and tell you where to find me,' he said. And then the car roared off.

No sooner had it disappeared around the corner than a police car came speeding from the opposite direction, tyres squealing. It pulled up in front of Makepeace. Lacey stared balefully at her from the back seat. 'Got anything to tell me, Sergeant?' he asked as he opened the door.

'I want to report a stolen car ...'

There were about a dozen people in the front room of the squat. All but one of them were teenagers or in their early twenties. The exception was Dempsey. He was playing a guitar and singing. 'It's a hard ... it's a hard ... it's a hard ... it's a hard ... It's a hard ra-ain, that's gonna fa-a-ll.'

He finished with a flourish on the guitar then put it down on the floor beside him. There was a murmur of approval from his young audience and the long-haired youth who'd been accompanying him on a mouth organ, said, 'My Dad taught me that song.'

'Thanks. That makes me feel old,' said Dempsey.

'Hey, I *like* older men,' said a dark-haired girl sitting beside Dempsey. She handed him a bottle of cider.

'Glad to hear it,' he told her then took a long drink from the bottle.

'How long have you been bummin' around, man?' asked the harmonica player.

'Not long.'

'Down on your luck?'

'And how,' agreed Dempsey. A joint that had been circulating around the group reached him. He passed it on without taking a drag.

The girl put her hand on his thigh and whispered in his ear, 'Want to come upstairs?'

'Upstairs?'

'Great view up there.'

Dempsey gave her an appreciative look. 'Yeah, I'll bet there is.'

At that moment Makepeace entered the room. She paused in the doorway for a moment until she spotted Dempsey then headed towards him. One of the youths gave her a long wolf-whistle . . .

'Come on, Dempsey, we have to talk,' she said, her expression grim.

'Sure, princess,' said Dempsey, getting up.

'Who's she?' asked the dark-haired girl.

'My mom . . .'

They went out into the darkened hallway. 'Sorry to

interrupt your party,' said Makepeace.

'It's cool, man. Don't worry, I won't tell them you're a cop.'

'Do they know *you're* a cop?'

'Nah. They think I'm a thief on the run.'

'Which you are. A car thief.' Makepeace held out her hand. Dempsey gave her the car keys.

'Where is it?'

'Just a few blocks from here. Unless the uniformed boys have spotted it.'

'For your sake I hope they haven't. So what did you get from Harris?'

Dempsey told her what Harris had said. She was thoughtful. 'You think Harris himself is mixed up in it?'

'I'd bet on it. But I can't prove it yet. It's just a ...'

'I know. A hunch.'

'The guy gives off bad vibes. A real smoothie on the surface but underneath ...' Dempsey shook his head.

'We need more than a hunch and bad vibes.'

'I know. What did you get from Embrey?'

'Not much. He did tell me Simmons didn't work on the building of the bank. He was still working at the quarry then.'

'Yeah? Tell me more about this quarry of Harris's.'

'Status symbol. All the biggest building firms buy their own quarries. Close to London, saves time. Bit of a heavy capital investment but it pays off in the long run. Harris bought it in 1981. Put Simmons in as Dispatcher. Three months later he was manager.'

'Fast mover.'

'Very. And less than two years later he had enough money to start up his own business. Something certainly smells. He was getting a lot of extra money from somewhere, that's for sure.'

'From Harris,' said Dempsey firmly.

'Yes, but *why*?'

'That's the million dollar question.'

Makepeace sighed. 'We're getting nowhere fast and time is running out. Sooner or later Lacey is going to find you. And probably sooner than later.'

'What did he say after I took off this afternoon?'

'Practically accused me of being your accomplice. But as he couldn't prove anything he had to let me go.'

'Hey, princess, I'm sorry I'm putting you through all this. I'll make it up to you when it's all over.'

'Really? How? By sending me a handmade mail bag from Wormwood Scrubs?'

'Don't be so negative.'

'It's hard not to be. What with my professional life in ruins and my love life going the same route ...'

'Lord Fawlty-towers still giving you a hard time?'

'Worse. He's given me an ultimatum. I've got to give him my decision tomorrow night instead of next week. His father, Lord Penward, is holding a party at his Mayfair house tomorrow night and Nigel wants to make the announcement then. To add to the agony my father's been invited too ...'

'So what are you gonna do? Marry the guy?'

Makepeace rubbed her temples with her fingertips. 'Please, Dempsey, don't ask me. I'm so mixed up at the moment I can't think properly. All this couldn't have happened at a worse time.'

Dempsey said nothing more. After a silence Makepeace said, 'What about you? Where are you going to stay tonight?'

'Here.'

'Here?' She wrinkled her nose.

'It's not so bad. The kids are okay and there are compensations.'

'Like what?'

'I'll tell you tomorrow,' he said and grinned.

Puzzled, she said, 'And what about tomorrow? What are you going to do?'

'I'm gonna get a job.'

She gave him a blank look. 'Really? What kind of job?'

'A job in a quarry.'

Chapter
TEN

Bob Malley was standing in the bed of the truck and smoothing out the fresh load of gravel with a shovel. The first he knew there was anyone behind him was when he heard an American voice say, 'Hey, are you Malley?'

Malley turned. He saw a tall man in his late thirties standing at the rear of the truck. He was unshaven and wearing gumboots, woollen cap and donkey jacket. Malley frowned at him. There was something about him that wasn't right but Malley couldn't put his finger on the reason. 'Yeah, I'm Malley,' he growled. 'Why?'

'Name's Jim Cooper. I'm the new driver. Guy in the office said you'd fix me up.'

'New driver, eh?' said Malley, still studying him. 'You any good?'

'Good enough.'

'Okay then. You can start with this load. Take it to

our Park Palace Hotel site in Princess Street. Know the one I mean?'

'Yeah, I know it.'

It was then that Malley recognised Dempsey.

As soon as Dempsey had driven the truck away Malley hurried to the Portakabin that served as his office and phoned Harris. 'Mr Harris, we got a problem.'

'Really?' said Harris, sounding unperturbed.

'Dempsey showed up here at the quarry. Got a job as a driver. I didn't recognise him at first, because of the beard he's growing. Calls himself Jim Cooper.'

'How very interesting.'

'What should I do?'

'I would think that's perfectly obvious. Kill him.'

'Hey, come on, Mr Harris. The guy's a cop! Why don't we just let Lacey know he's here?'

'Because it's quite likely that Dempsey would give Lacey the slip yet again. And I can't afford to have that happen. Dempsey is starting to dig a little too deep. I want him out of the way, for good.'

'But a cop ...'

'He's an ex-cop as far as the Force is concerned. And a dirty one to boot. They're not going to care if he conveniently gets himself killed. Especially if it looks like an accident.'

'Well ...' said Malley, dubiously. 'I guess so ...'

'Deal with it as soon as possible. Where is Dempsey now?'

'I sent him out with a load. What kind of accident have you got in mind?'

'I'll leave it up to you. Use your imagination. After all, quarries are dangerous places ...'

Malley nodded. 'Yeah, they sure are, Mr Harris.'

The transport café, in the Ruislip Road less than half a mile from the Harris-Strang quarry, was full even though it was only half-past eleven in the morning. Dempsey, seated in a corner, was working his way through a mixed grill of epic proportions. He was so pre-occupied with his food that he didn't see Makepeace enter the café. It was only when he heard the chorus of wolf whistles that greeted her entrance that he looked up and saw her approaching his table.

'Hi, princess. I saved you a seat. Sit down.'

The wolf whistles continued as she sat down. Her stony expression told Dempsey she was hating every moment of it and he couldn't really blame her.

'You really do pick the loveliest places for our meetings, Dempsey,' she said tersely.

'I'm a trucker, ain't I? And this is a truckers' café so ergo I eat here. Actually, I kinda like it. Got atmosphere.'

'That's the smell of burning fat.'

Dempsey laughed. 'Come on, loosen up, princess.'

'It's all right for you in here, Dempsey. You're a man. I, on the other hand, am a woman and I don't particularly enjoy sitting here being mentally undressed and having my anatomy discussed by a bunch of morons.'

Dempsey glanced around and saw that she was right. She was being leered at by every man in the place and there were whispered comments going back and forth followed by sniggers. He said, 'Well, this won't take long ...'

'Good. Spikings thinks I'm meeting a grass who's

got something on the Holdstock case. What have you got?'

'This ...' He put his knife and fork down and then put his hands in his jacket pockets. From his left hand he then poured a heap of gravel on the table in front of Makepeace, and from his right hand he poured a small pile of sand. Makepeace looked at the two mounds then back at Dempsey. 'What are they?'

'That one is sand,' said Dempsey, pointing. 'And that one is gravel.'

'Now I know how Watson must have felt. Such powers of detection are almost supernatural.'

'I want them analysed.'

'Analysed?'

'Both samples came from the Harris-Strang quarry. I want them analysed.'

'You brought me all the way out here for a handful of sand and gravel?'

'And lunch. You want me to order you something?'

She reached across the table, picked up the sauce container shaped like a tomato and squeezed its contents over the remains of Dempsey's meal.

He looked at the mass of tomato sauce and said, 'It's okay, I like a lot of catsup. Now can you get that stuff analysed as soon as possible?'

She sighed. 'You really think it's important?'

'Could be where the scam is. Maybe it's some kind of rich mineral deposit or some such. Something that Simmons found out about and used as a hold over Harris.'

'Very well. Give me your cap.'

Dempsey frowned but took off his cap and handed it to her. She scooped the mounds of sand and gravel into it, folded it up and put it in her shoulder bag. 'Keep in touch,' she told him. 'And take care ...' She got up and headed for the door. Once again she provoked a chorus of wolf whistles, accompanied this time by some particularly coarse comments. She walked all the way to the door but instead of opening it she stopped and then whirled round. At the same time she drew her .32 revolver from inside her jacket.

Total silence descended on the café. Makepeace waved the gun about in a low arc, covering the truck drivers at crotch level. She said coldly, 'The next one of you to make a sound will get a piece of lead through his Y-fronts. Any takers?'

No one made a sound.

Satisfied, Makepeace holstered her gun and marched out of the café.

The silence continued for a time after she'd gone then, one by one, the truckers began to turn and stare questioningly at Dempsey.

He shrugged and said, 'Hey guys, what can I say? She's my ex-wife and whenever I get behind on my alimony payments she gets a little touchy . . .'

When Dempsey drove the truck back into the quarry he saw that Malley was waiting for him.

'Slow run, Cooper,' Malley called to him as he braked to a stop.

'I took my lunch break a bit early. Is that okay?'

Malley scowled. 'I dunno if you got what it takes, Cooper, so I'm going to put you through our test circuit.'

'Test circuit? The guy who hired me didn't say nothing about a test circuit.'

'Yeah, well *I* am. New boys always do the circuit. We find out if they can drive in all conditions.'

'I can.'

'Well, I'm gonna be the judge of that.' Malley came round to the passenger side of the truck's cab and climbed in. 'Start 'er up. I'll tell you where to go ...'

Dempsey had no choice but to obey. At the back of his mind a small warning bell had started to ring.

Malley directed him to the quarry wasteland at the rear of the quarry pit itself. It was like a lunar landscape with British weather. A sea of mud consisting of high mounds and deep craters. The only sign of movement in this bleak setting was a large bulldozer creating yet another mound of quarry waste in the distance. A second, stationary, bulldozer stood empty nearby like a sleeping prehistoric monster.

'Okay, this is what you do,' said Malley, getting out of the truck. 'You drive straight through all that 'til you reach the fence, then you go to the right, follow the fence 'til you reach the east corner. Then you come back along the edge of the pit.' He pointed. 'See the track?'

'Yeah, I see it,' said Dempsey. 'That's all I gotta do? Take it around one time?'

'Think you can handle it?'

Dempsey's suspicions were fading away. It looked simple. 'No problem, buddy.' He revved up the motor then sent the truck lurching forward.

It was a rough, bone-shaking ride to the fence and at times Dempsey had trouble keeping control of the truck as it slid about in the mud but he'd driven in worse conditions and was confident he would make it.

Things improved a little when he reached the fence and turned right along it but he knew he still had the most difficult stretch to come.

And he was right. The track alongside the pit was a muddy nightmare and Dempsey had to use all his driving skills to avoid getting bogged down.

He was concentrating so hard on his driving that he didn't see the approaching bulldozer until it was too late. The big machine, its heavy blade parallel with the ground, came trundling down the side of a mound with the obvious aim of slamming broadside into Dempsey's truck.

Dempsey tried to put on a burst of speed but it was no use. The truck could go no faster through the glue-like mud. The blade of the bulldozer slammed into the side of the truck with an echoing clang. Dempsey found himself staring face-to-face at the driver who was a heavily-built skinhead. The skinhead grinned at him. The truck began to slip sideways.

Dempsey glanced out the window. The edge of the quarry pit was about eight feet away ...

He put his foot down on the accelerator but he could feel the truck's rear wheels spinning uselessly in the mud. He looked back at the skinhead, wishing he had his gun. The truck was sliding faster now. He knew he had only seconds left ...

He dived for the passenger door, flung it open and saw the long drop into the pit below him. Hanging onto the open door he pulled himself out of the cab then scrambled round onto the hood.

The side of the truck now hung suspended over the edge of the pit. Then Dempsey felt it start to topple sideways. He launched himself into the air ...

With a screech of protesting metal the truck rolled over the edge of the quarry. At that same moment Dempsey landed, hard, in the mud. Winded, he lay there for a few seconds, listening to the sounds the truck made as it bounced down the side of the quarry.

Another, nearer, sound made him glance over his shoulder. The bulldozer had swung round now and was advancing on him. The blade was being raised and he realized the driver intended to squash him under it . . .

Dempsey got to his knees and started to crawl. The roar of the bulldozer's engine was so loud it almost drowned out the dull explosion that signalled the truck's destruction on the floor of the quarry.

He tried to stand and run but slipped in the treacherous mud and fell face down again. Instinctively, he clawed himself forward, pulling his legs up under him . . .

There was a loud thud behind him. He looked and saw that the huge blade had come down hard, digging deep into the mud. If he hadn't moved when he did he would have had both legs chopped off at the knee.

Dempsey got up again and staggered forward, slipping and sliding as he went. He had to reach high ground . . .

He started up the side of a mound, the bulldozer close behind him. If he could reach the top he could pick up speed sliding down the other side and put some distance between himself and his pursuer . . .

He fell again and started to slide backwards towards the bulldozer climbing the mound behind him. Dempsey swore and dug the toes of his boots into the mud. He stopped sliding. A glance over his shoulder told him the machine was gaining on him. Its great blade was rising into the air again . . .

Dempsey frantically increased his efforts and managed to scramble to the top of the mound. Then he saw something that raised his hopes. The second bulldozer. It stood at the base of the mound less than a dozen yards away.

He didn't hesitate. He flung himself forward and let himself tumble and slide down the muddy slope until he hit the bottom. Then he sprang to his feet and clambered onto the bulldozer.

The keys weren't in the dashboard but, Dempsey told himself, you can't have everything . . .

He reached under and pulled out the ignition wires. He wrenched them apart then 'hotwired' the bulldozer's powerful engine into growling life. He looked back. The other machine was just breasting the top of the mound.

Dempsey turned his attention to the controls. It had been years since he had driven anything like this massive earth-mover. In fact the last time had been just after he'd been kicked out of high school and got a job up near Buffalo working on the building of a new freeway but he remembered enough to be confident he could handle the machine . . .

Instead of a steering wheel there were two levers that controlled the two caterpillar treads. To turn the bulldozer, say, to the right, you stopped the right tread while accelerating the left, and vice versa for turning left . . .

Dempsey set the machine rumbling forward then slewed it round sharply to meet the other bulldozer that was coming down the side of the mound. At the same time he raised his blade . . .

The blades met with a bone rattling *clang* that made the fillings in Dempsey's teeth vibrate painfully. For several minutes Dempsey and the skinhead indulged in a mechanical duel, using the giant blades of their machines as ponderous, slow-moving fencing weapons, but neither of them could gain the advantage.

Dempsey, realizing he couldn't win against someone who was so much more experienced than him in the use of such machines decided that a change of tactics was called for . . .

Disengaging from the duel he turned his machine and headed towards the pit. The skinhead, sensing imminent victory, gave chase.

Dempsey turned sharply round a heap of quarry waste then dug his blade deep into the grey sludge. When he'd forced as much as he could into the scoop he raised it as high as possible above his machine. Then he turned his bulldozer round to meet his pursuer head on.

The skinhead frowned when he saw Dempsey waiting there apparently defenceless with his blade raised overhead. Then, obviously deciding he couldn't let the opportunity go to waste he charged . . .

Dempsey waited until almost the last moment then turned the lever that swivelled the scoop forward . . .

The skinhead looked up in time to see the ton and a half of grey mud and sludge descending towards him. He screamed and threw his machine into reverse but it too late. The grey mass thudded down on both him and the machine, cutting his scream off with an unsettling abruptness.

Where the skinhead had been sitting was now a great, grey mound of mud but the machine continued to move backwards. There was nothing Dempsey could do to stop it. Even if he could get on board it the controls would be out of reach under all that sludge. So he sat there and watched helplessly as the machine backed towards the edge of the pit.

The end was very quick. One moment the bulldozer was tilting backwards on the edge, its giant blade swinging upwards, and the next moment both it and a large section of the pit edge had vanished from sight. Then came a loud rumble from the bottom of the pit.

For several seconds Dempsey sat paralysed with

shock but a shout behind him broke the spell. he turned and saw the unmistakable bulk of Malley heading towards him. He was followed by two other men. All three were carrying pickaxe handles ...

Chapter
ELEVEN

'Mr Malley is on line two, sir,' announced Harris's secretary over the intercom. Harris picked up the phone. 'Hello, Malley. I trust you have good news for me.'

There was silence on the other end of the line and just as Harris was beginning to think the connection had been broken Malley said, 'Uh, things didn't go exactly as, er, planned, Mr Harris.'

It was Harris's turn to be silent.

'Mr Harris?'

'I'm here. Go on, Malley.'

'Uh, well, we lost Slater.'

'*We* did, did *we*? And how did *we* manage that?' asked Harris, his tone ominous.

'Dempsey wasted him.' Malley then proceeded to describe what had happened. When he'd finished, Harris said bleakly, 'And then I trust you took care of the Lieutenant?'

There was another silence. 'Er, well, we tried, Mr Harris. But the bastard got away. In the JCB. He drove it right through the fence out along the Ruislip Road ...'

'He ... did ... *what*?'

'Caused a hell of a lot of problems. Traffic jams and everything. By the time we got there he'd scarpered, leaving the JCB right in the middle of the road, blocking both lanes ... and then the bloody filth arrive, don't they ...'

'What did you tell them?'

'Well, I couldn't say it was Dempsey, could I? Lacey would wonder what he was up to at the quarry. So I told the local cops he was some drunken paddy we'd just hired who'd gone crazy. Gave 'em a fake name and description too ... did I do right, Mr Harris?'

'Oh, yes, you did *right*, Malley,' said Harris, sarcastically. 'Apart from losing a JCB, a truck and Slater, not to mention Dempsey himself. I'm beginning to wonder if you're worth the money I pay you.'

'It won't happen again. Mr Harris. I'm gonna get that Yank bastard. It's *personal* now. He made me look a right idiot ...'

'He obviously didn't have to try very hard,' snarled Harris. 'So tell me just *how* you're going to get him? Did he leave a business card? Did you arrange to meet for a pint after work? Or have you suddenly developed psychic powers, Malley?'

'Uhhh ...' said Malley.

'You can say that again,' said Harris and slammed the phone down in disgust. He heaved his huge body out of his chair and went to the window. As he stared out over London he rubbed his chin reflectively. There *had* to be a way of flushing Dempsey out before he could get too near to the truth.

Makepeace emerged from the Holborn Central police station with an angry look on her face. She marched to her car, got in and slammed the door. Then she drove off with a squeal of rubber.

'Why so pissed off, princess?' asked a voice close behind her. She gave a start of surprise and almost collided with a cyclist she was overtaking. She avoided hitting him with split seconds to spare. He raised his fist and shook it at her.

'Dempsey!' she cried. 'You almost got us killed!'

He leaned over the back of the passenger seat and grinned at her. His face and beard were spattered with mud. She glanced briefly at him and asked, 'How on earth did you find me?'

'I had a hunch you'd turn up at Holborn Central. Lacey been chewin' you out again?'

'Yes. Gave me my one last chance to come clean and confess that I've been helping you and that I know where you are. Said if I did he'd put in a good word on my behalf with both the Divisional Commander and God.'

'God?'

'Didn't I tell you? Lacey and God are a double-act, at least as far as Lacey is concerned. He checks out everything with God beforehand ... then he acts.'

'Uh-oh, that sounds bad. I've met types like that before. You can't argue with them.'

'Well, you certainly can't argue with Lacey, as I keep finding out to my cost. But you took an awful chance sneaking into my car when it was parked right outside Holborn Central.'

'No choice. I had to talk to you. Things are hotting up.'

'What do you mean?'

'I lost my job. The foreman at the quarry gave me my walking papers ...'

She gave him a puzzled glance. 'Is that all?'

'Well, it's the *way* he gave me my walking papers. He had a guy in a bulldozer try and shove the truck I was driving off the edge of the quarry. I didn't want to be made *that* redundant so I got kind of mad, then I quit.'

She looked at him again. 'Give me the full story,' she said. He did so.

'You were lucky,' she told him. 'Very.'

'Hey, give me some credit. It was more skill than luck.'

'Whatever. But it does mean we're getting close.'

'Yeah, *I* am, ain't I? What about the stuff I gave you? Did you get it analysed?'

'The sand was sand and ...'

He groaned. 'Don't tell me. The gravel was gravel.'

'Gravel that contains opal particles.'

'Opal ...?!' he said excitedly.

'Calm down. Not gem-grade. Valueless. The quarry is a quarry is a quarry.'

'So we're still nowhere,' Dempsey sighed.

'I wouldn't say that. The foreman of the quarry tried to have you killed. That certainly proves something, apart from your usual lack of popularity.'

'Yeah,' agreed Dempsey. 'Which suggests he could have been the same guy who hit Simmons. But what we need to find out is *why*.'

'Well, good luck. I wish I could help some more but I have to take the night off.'

'What?'

'I told you. I have to go to this party being held by Nigel's father. I can't get out of it.'

'Well, I sure wouldn't want our efforts to clear my name to interfere with your social life, princess,' he said dryly. 'You go ahead and enjoy yourself. Don't worry about me. I'll get by.'

'Dempsey, you *know* how important tonight is for me.'

'Yeah,' he grunted. 'Don't forget to give Lord Flauntalot my regards.'

'Dempsey . . .'

'How about dropping me off near the squat. While you're hitting the champagne and caviar set tonight I've got a lot of thinking to do, and I might as well get started now . . .'

Several hours later Dempsey was ready to admit defeat. He had been lying on a sleeping bag in one of the top rooms of the squat and running the problems of Simmons, the bank, Harris and his quarry through his mind over and over again. He had tried every possible permutation but he just couldn't see what the common link might be. And yet at the same time he got the feeling the solution was staring him in the face.

There was a light tap at the door. 'Yeah?' he growled, annoyed at being disturbed. The door opened and the young, dark-haired girl slipped quietly into the room. 'Oh, hi, Alison,' he said, a shade more friendly.

'You okay, Jim?' she asked, sounding concerned. 'You've been up here by yourself an awfully long time. I was thinking you might be sick.'

'Nah,' he said. 'Just needed to be alone. Had some things to sort out in my mind . . .'

'You get them sorted out?'

110

He grunted. 'Not by a long shot.'

'Well, if you still want to be by yourself ...' she said, and started to back away.

'Hey, no. I'm all through thinking for the night. My mind is tied up in knots. I could do with some company.'

Very quickly, she joined him on the sleeping bag. She cuddled up close to him and kissed him lightly on the mouth. 'It was good last night, wasn't it?' she whispered.

'What?' said Dempsey, his thoughts still in other areas. 'Oh, yeah. Yeah, it was ...'

'How long are you going to stay here, Jim?'

'I dunno. Could be a coupla more days. Could be longer.'

'It can't be *too* much longer,' she said as she ran her fingers through his hair.

'Um? Why not?'

'Didn't you know? This place gets torn down early next week. Going to be demolished right down to the ground. They're going to build a luxury block of flats here.'

'Yeah?' said Dempsey. In his mind's eye he could see a wrecking ball on the end of a chain crashing through the masonry, followed by men with sledge-hammers and pickaxes attacking the loosened brick-work.

'I'll probably head south,' said Alison. 'Maybe go to Brighton and bum around. Soon be spring and the weather should start getting better.'

'Yeah ...' said Dempsey, unable to get the image of the demolition workers out of his mind.

'So I was thinking,' continued Alison, 'that maybe you'd like to come with me, Jim. Would you like that? We could have a lot of fun ...'

Suddenly the pieces all fell together in Dempsey's head. He sat up suddenly and cried. 'Got it!'

Alison, startled, said, 'Got what?'

'The *answer*, I hope!' He leapt to his feet and headed for the door.

'Wait! Where are you going?' she cried.

'To see a lady about a bank!'

'But what about Brighton ...? By then Dempsey was already running down the stairs.

'You're looking absolutely gorgeous,' Nigel Penward told Makepeace enthusiastically. 'And that dress is breath-taking.'

She accepted the compliment with a distracted nod, her mind obviously on other matters. They were standing in the drawing room of Lord Penward's spacious Georgian town house which was rapidly filling up with guests for the party.

'So what's your decision?' Nigel asked her.

'What?' she said and took an absent-minded sip of her champagne.

'About the wedding, darling. *Our* wedding. Father really would like to make the announcement at some point during this bash. Preferably when Charles and Diana are here.'

'Who?'

He sighed with exasperation. 'Charles and Diana. I told you there's a fifty-fifty chance they might turn up.'

'Oh yes,' she said. 'You did. That's nice.'

'Harriet, what *is* the matter with you tonight?'

'I've got a lot on my mind. Problems.'

'So it seems. But what about your decision?'

'What?'

112

'Good grief, Harriet, snap out of it!' he said, raising his voice. 'Your decision about our marriage!'

'Oh yes,' she said wearily. 'That's one of my problems.'

At that moment Lord Winfield, Makepeace's father, appeared and she turned to him gratefully. 'Hullo, Daddy ... enjoying yourself?'

Lord Winfield, a large glass of brandy in his hand, said, 'Very much so, Harry. Very much so.' Then he leaned toward her and said in a loud whisper, 'I say, when is the big announcement going to be made?'

Makepeace winced. 'Oh, not you too, Daddy.'

'Harriet is still prevaricating on the matter, Lord Winfield,' said Nigel.

Lord Winfield looked surprised. 'Really? But your father told me it was all cut and dried.'

'I wish people would ask *me* first before they make plans about my future,' said Makepeace angrily.

'Er ... excuse me, madam ...' It was one of Lord Winfield's footmen. 'There's er ... a *gentleman* asking for you at the front entrance. Said it's urgent. I told him you couldn't be disturbed but he's being very insistent ...'

'Who is he?' asked Makepeace, frowning. Then she heard Nigel groan. She turned and saw Dempsey, still in his mud-spattered working clothes, striding purposefully towards her through the throng of dinner-suited and begowned guests. 'Oh God ...' she sighed. He was also carrying a large, dirty tool bag.

Dempsey grinned at her. 'Hi, princess. I got a question for you. How long's it take two guys with hand tools to break through twelve feet of reinforced concrete?'

Before Makepeace could say anything Nigel stepped between them. 'Are you mad?!' he cried at

Dempsey. 'What the hell are you doing here?'

Dempsey gripped him by both shoulders and moved him to one side as if he was a clothing store dummy. 'What about that question, princess?' Dempsey asked her. 'Got an answer yet?'

'Shall I have him thrown out, madam?' enquired the footman calmly. Dempsey glared at him. 'How'd you like a caviar spoon shoved up your nose?'

Lord Winfield, who'd been watching the proceedings with a bemused expression until then, suddenly gave Dempsey a beaming smile. 'Why, it's James Dempsey, isn't it? Underneath all that face fungus. I thought I recognised you!' He held out his hand. Dempsey shook it. 'Hi ya, Lord Winfield. Nice to see ya again.'

Nigel Penward stared at Lord Winfield in astonishment. 'You mean to say you *know* this revolting specimen?!'

'Why, of course I do. James saved my bacon last year, with a little help from Harry too ...'

'It was more than a *little* help,' muttered Makepeace.

'Close thing though, wasn't it, James?' said Lord Winfield jovially. 'If you hadn't located that Chinese jade collection I might have ended up behind bars ...'

Nigel shook his head with disbelief. 'I'm dreaming all this. It's a bad dream ...'

'I must be having the same one,' said Makepeace.

'Harriet, you've *got* to get rid of him! What if Charles and Diana were to arrive while he was still here? I mean, *look* at him!'

'Charles and Diana?' asked Dempsey. 'Hey, no kidding! I'd like to meet them!'

Nigel threw up his hands in disgust and walked off. Makepeace said, 'Dempsey, do you spend hours

114

every day thinking up ways of ruining my life?'

'Come on, princess, this is important. I think I got the answer to the whole problem.'

She frowned at him. 'Yes . . .?'

'The concrete, princess, the concrete! At the bank! Remember my question?'

The light began to dawn in her eyes. Slowly she said, 'The bank was open Saturday morning. They couldn't have had more than . . . what? Three hours?'

Dempsey grinned at her. 'Four tops, I figure.'

'Then . . .'

'Yeah.' He jiggled the tool bag. There was the clank of metal on metal. 'That's why I bought these. Digging tools. We're gonna break into a bank vault tonight, princess. The same one that Simmons got into . . .'

She stared at him. 'Are you serious?'

'Perfectly.'

'You expect me — dressed like this — to help you rob a bank?'

He shrugged. 'You can take it off if you like. Hey, isn't it the same dress you wore to Chas's wedding?'

'It's the same dress I *didn't* wear to Chas's wedding. But I'm surprised you recognised it without the mud stains.'

'Er, excuse me for butting in,' said Lord Winfield, who had been listening to their conversation with increasing bewilderment. 'But tell me, James, are you on some special undercover case? I was wondering about your disguise.'

'That's not a disguise, Daddy. That's Dempsey's New Look. Early primitive. It's all the rage these days,' Makepeace told her father.

'Really?' he said, appearing even more bewildered.

'Are you coming?' Dempsey asked Makepeace.

'There's got to be two of us using the tools to prove my theory.'

'No. I am definitely not helping you rob a bank tonight. Some other time, perhaps.'

Nigel returned, his expression sour. 'He's still here, I see,' he said, indicating Dempsey.

'Unfortunately, yes,' said Makepeace.

'Well, he won't be for much longer. I've just called the police. They're on their way . . .'

Chapter

TWELVE

'You did *what*?' asked Makepeace, shocked.

'I called the police,' repeated Nigel defiantly. 'This ridiculous situation has gone on long enough, Harriet. Someone's got to save you from yourself as you obviously don't have the sense to do it.'

'You . . . you . . . *bastard*,' she told him.

'I'll second that,' said Dempsey calmly as he lifted a chicken leg from a tray being carried by a passing waiter.

Nigel's eyes had widened with surprise. 'But Harriet, I did it for your sake. Don't you understand . . . ?'

She shook her head. 'God, what a fool I've been.'

Nigel brightened. 'Well, I'm glad you're beginning to see sense, Harriet . . .'

'To think I even seriously contemplated marrying you for a single second, much less for over two months . . . I must have been mad.'

'Attaboy, princess,' said Dempsey, his mouth full of chicken.

'What?!' gasped Nigel, staring at her in disbelief. 'Harriet, you can't mean it!'

'Oh, yes I do!' She turned to Dempsey. 'Come on, let's go to work.'

Lord Winfield, now looking very bewildered indeed, said, 'I'm not following any of this, I don't think ... Nigel has called the police, and yet you two *are* the police ... and now you're saying you don't want to marry him ...' He shook his head. 'Does this mean the wedding's off?'

'It does indeed, Daddy,' said Makepeace firmly.

'But ... but ...' protested Nigel, his mouth opening and closing like a goldfish.

'Let's get going,' said Makepeace, grasping Dempsey by the elbow and leading him away.

'Wait, Harry!' cried Lord Winfield. 'Where are you going now?'

'To break into a bank vault,' she called over her shoulder.

'Oh ... I see,' said Lord Winfield, nodding.

But as Dempsey and Makepeace hurried towards the front hall they heard the sound of police cars pulling up outside. 'That's torn it,' said Makepeace.

'Quick, which way to the kitchens?' Dempsey asked her.

She pointed. 'Why?'

'I got an idea. You head for the bank on your own. If I get out I'll meet you there. If I don't, start baking lots of cakes with files in 'em ...'

As Dempsey entered the kitchen area he was stopped by a large, plump man dressed entirely in white. 'And where do you think *you're* going?' he demanded of Dempsey.

Dempsey gave the man a quick flash of his S.I.10 ID. 'Special Investigator for the Health Department,' he said. 'I'm here to give your facilities a spot check and to talk to your staff.'

The plump man stared in amazement at Dempsey. 'You're a ... a health inspector?' He flared his nostrils with disdain. 'But you're *filthy*.'

'I told you — I'm a Special Investigator. We always work in disguise like this. You must have encountered one of us before this.'

The man looked doubtful. 'I don't think so ...'

'Yeah?' Dempsey frowned. 'That's not good. May work against you in my report ...'

'But this is a *private* residence,' protested the man.

'That may be so but you get a lot of guests coming here for meals. Take tonight. You got Chuck — I mean Charles — and Diana dropping in for a snack, right?'

'Well, yes ...'

'That's why I'm here.' He looked at his watch. 'C'mon, I don't have much time. First I got to interview one of your waiters. In private.' He stared around at the waiters coming in and out of the kitchen, looking for one roughly his same size.

'But I don't understand why ...'

'It's not your job to understand why,' said Dempsey roughly. 'Just as long as I do.' He jabbed a finger at a well-built waiter who had just entered the kitchen. 'That guy, I'll talk to him. Call him over.'

The plump man beckoned to the waiter. 'Harry, this man is a ... a health inspector. He wants to talk to you.'

'Privately,' added Dempsey. 'Where can we go?'

The plump man thought then said, 'You can use the staff changing room. Harry, show him where it is ...'

'The staff changing room sounds perfect,' said Dempsey as he followed the puzzled-looking Harry out of the kitchen.

A short time later Dempsey emerged from the changing room wearing Harry's uniform. The first person he encountered was a uniformed constable but he walked past Dempsey without a second glance.

Dempsey hurried on. Spotting a waiter carrying a tray-load of full champagne glasses he went up to him, took the tray out of his hands before he could protest and said, 'I'm relieving you, bud. Take a rest break ...'

As Dempsey headed back towards the front of the building he saw that the place was crawling with police, both uniformed and plainclothed, though both equally distinctive. Lacey obviously meant business this time.

Then Dempsey saw Lacey himself. He was deep in conversation with Nigel Penward who was looking very unhappy. Holding the tray higher so that it obscured the lower part of his face Dempsey walked right past them and kept heading for the front door. Then, out of the corner of his eye, he saw Detective Sergeant Taylor moving to intercept him. Dempsey's stomach muscles tightened unpleasantly as Taylor approached, but to his surprise Taylor merely lifted one of the glasses of champagne from the tray and walked away.

Dempsey continued on to the lobby, slipped easily through the cordon of uniformed police officers waiting there and then strode towards the front door. He was just opening it when a footman — the same footman he'd encountered earlier — said testily, 'Where on earth do you think you're going with those drinks, man?'

'Lord Penward's instructions, sir,' Dempsey told him.

'Instructions? What instructions? Why are you taking that champagne *outside?*'

As Dempsey desperately tried to think of a reason he saw a black Rolls Royce glide to a halt in front of the house. The Rolls was displaying a Royal Pennant. Without a second's hesitation Dempsey told the footman, 'It's for them ...' Then he hurried down the steps. As the chauffeur opened the rear door Dempsey did a deep bow from the waist and offered the tray with the words, 'Have a drink, your Highnesses. On the house.'

Half an hour later Dempsey was outside the newspaper shop adjacent to the Frith and Hanway bank. He looked around for Makepeace but there was no sign of her. But then, to his relief, he saw her car emerge from the shadows of a side street and stop at the corner. He went over to it. 'Hi, princess. You have any trouble getting away?'

She shook her head. 'How about you? Or are you dressed as a waiter just for the hell of it?'

Dempsey told her how he got out of Lord Penward's house. '... And when Chuck and Di arrived it was the perfect distraction. I could have dropped my pants and no one would have paid me a bit of notice.'

'You resisted the temptation, I trust?' Makepeace said dryly.

'All I did was escort them up to the front door. That was after I gave them the drinks in the car ...'

Makepeace stared at him. 'You gave them drinks before they even got out of their *car*?'

'Yeah. Sure. They seemed to think it was pretty funny.'

'I'm sure they did.'

'Anyway, they go in and I just slipped away. No problem.'

'Dempsey, you never cease to amaze me — unfortunately.'

'You bring the tools?'

She passed him the bag. He took out a crowbar. 'I'll go open the door. You stay here and keep watch. When I signal, come running.'

'I can't run in these shoes and this gown.'

'Well, waddle fast ...' Dempsey hurried back to the shop doorway and got to work trying to jemmy the door open. He hadn't been at it long when a police constable on the beat suddenly appeared. There was no time for Makepeace to give Dempsey a warning so she sat there watching helplessly ...

'What do you think you're up to, sunshine?' demanded the constable.

Dempsey turned in surprise, trying to conceal the crowbar. 'Oh, 'ullo, officer,' he said in a bad imitation of a cockney accent. 'I was just ... just ... er ...'

'Doing a bit of breaking and entering, right?'

'No, no, nuffink like that, guvnor,' Dempsey protested.

'The question is, sunshine, why are you trying to break into an empty shop? You're either a very stupid burglar or you know something I don't know. Which is it?'

'Really, guvnor ... I can explain everything. You

see I'm a plasterer by trade and a couple of days ago I was working in this shop and I happened to leave behind my ... my wallet ... and ...'

'If you're a plasterer why are you dressed as a waiter?'

'Uh ... that's my night job. Yeah. I'm a plasterer by day and waiter by night. Got a lot of kids to support ...'

The constable stepped closer to him and peered hard into his face. 'Stop talking rubbish and give me your name. I think I know you from somewhere.'

'Somewhere? Never been there, guvnor.'

'I definitely know your face.' He grabbed Dempsey by the arm. 'Drop that crowbar, that's a good lad.' He applied pressure and Dempsey did as he was told. 'Now tell me your name.'

'Cooper. Jim Cooper.'

The constable switched on his 2-way radio and was about to call in to his station when Makepeace tapped him on the shoulder. 'Don't do that, constable.'

He turned and his mouth opened in surprise when he saw an attractive blonde wearing a low cut evening gown standing there with a .32 revolver in her hand. 'What the ...?' he began.

She held out her S.I.10 ID card. 'Don't they ever brief you wallies?' she asked briskly.

The constable looked even more confused. He peered about worriedly and said, 'Is this a special ...?'

'It is. Or rather it *was*. It isn't anymore, thanks to your size twelves. Do you realize how long this operation took to set up?'

'I'm sorry, miss ... I ... I ...'

'It's *sergeant*, constable. And you can go now. I'll take care of him.' She was pointing the gun at Dempsey.

123

'Er, want me to call in for you?' the constable asked her hesitantly.

'No. My back-up unit is on its way. You've done enough damage. Go and try some door handles.'

With a final, curious glance at Dempsey the constable went on his way. When he'd turned the corner Dempsey said, 'Nice work, partner.'

She shrugged. 'I've dug my professional grave so deep a few more feet don't matter at this stage. Besides, I couldn't bear to hear that ridiculous accent of yours a moment longer.'

'I thought it was pretty good. Pure cockney.'

'Pure Hollywood. You sounded like Dick Van Dyke in *Mary Poppins*.'

'I've never seen *Mary Poppins*, princess. Not my kind of movie.'

'No. I imagine not.'

He picked up the crowbar and resumed prising open the door. 'I still think it was a good accent . . .'

Makepeace took another hard swing at the chisel with her hammer but all she succeeded in doing was dislodging a cloud of dust which settled over her like a white mist. She coughed and blew the hair out of her eyes. 'Tell me again about this brilliant theory of yours, Dempsey.'

'Stand back, I'm going to have a try with this.'

She stepped away from the bank vault wall as Dempsey swung the sledge-hammer at the concrete. There was a loud crunch and a few more fragments fell from the small hole that it had taken him nearly half an hour to produce.

'I don't understand,' he said, panting. 'This concrete is as hard as . . .'

'Concrete,' said Makepeace.

He dropped the sledge-hammer and slumped against the wall. 'I guess you can't dig through a bank wall in four hours. So how did Simmons and his pal do it . . .?'

Makepeace frowned. Then she took her chisel and hammer to a different section of the bank wall. She put the point of the chisel against the concrete and swung the hammer. The chisel sunk at least two inches into the concrete.

'Wha . . .?' said Dempsey, mystified.

She grinned at him. 'It just occurred to me — we've been working on the new section of the wall. It's made of different concrete to the older parts — the old concrete that Simmons and friend got through so quickly.'

Dempsey scooped up his sledge-hammer, ran over and swung it against the wall with all his strength. A veritable crater appeared with the impact. 'It's cheesecake!' he exclaimed in wonder. 'I was right!'

'Yes.' Makepeace dropped her hammer and chisel. 'You've proved your point. Now let's get out of here.'

But he continued to stare at the hole he'd made in the bank wall. 'You realize how close we are to a hell of a lot of bread, princess?'

'Who cares? Let's go.'

'Don't rush me. Ever think about how we spend our lives? Bustin' our guts for no thanks at all. Having to kow-tow to creeps like Lacey . . . Think what we could do with all that money in there.'

'Yes. We could use it to hire a good lawyer — which we would very definitely need. Come on, Dempsey . . .'

'I'm telling you I've had a bellyful. All the years I've been a cop and when the crunch comes I'm thrown to the wolves. Why shouldn't I help myself? I could be through that mush in a coupla hours.'

'Dempsey, I'll pretend I'm not hearing any of this. Will you please come with me . . . *now*!!'

But Dempsey continued to stare at the bank wall with an expression that she had never seen before. Then, suddenly, his face softened and he grinned at her. 'Good thing I'm an honest cop, ain't it?'

'Phew,' she said. 'You really had me worried then.'

'*You* were worried? Hell, so was *I*.'

As they drove away from the bank Dempsey held up a handful of the concrete they'd collected as evidence and said, 'We gotta get this analysed, but fast.'

'And how are we going to manage that at *this* time of night?'

'There's a guy I know — geologist. He's helped out forensic before. Genius at pinpointing the origin of soil and mineral samples. He might be able to help us . . . I met him once, on the Pringle case. He was able to prove that Pringle had been murdered in the grounds of that drug-smuggler's mansion in Cornwall by analysing the traces of mud on Pringle's shoes.'

'And what's the name of this genius?'

'Hang on, I'm trying to remember. It's a funny name. Guy's a foreigner.' Dempsey frowned with concentration.

'You mean he's an American?'

'No. He's a *foreign* foreigner . . . Aha!' He snapped his fingers. 'Got it! His name is Vahimagi. Doctor Taas Vahimagi. Stop at the next phone box you see and I'll check him out in the phone book. Can't be many Vahimagis listed . . .'

'I should think not,' agreed Makepeace.

* * *

'Got the address,' said Dempsey as he climbed back into the car. 'Lives in Kensington. 'Bout ten minutes drive from here ... Get on to the Cromwell Road and I'll give you directions from there.'

'I doubt if he's going to be very pleased to see us,' said Makepeace as she pulled away from the kerb.

'Can't be helped. If he can confirm what we already suspect about this concrete then I'm home free. And the first thing I'm gonna do is make Lacey eat a ton of the stuff.'

They drove on in silence for a time then Dempsey said, 'Hey, princess, about tonight. I'm sorry if I screwed things up between you and What's-his-name.'

'I don't want to talk about it, Dempsey,' she said firmly.

'That's cool. I understand.' He paused then added, 'But you gotta admit that marrying that jerk would have been the biggest mistake of your life.'

'Dempsey!'

'Sorry.'

Then, after another stretch of silence, Makepeace said, 'I will admit you were right about one thing about Nigel.'

'Yeah? What's that?'

'I hadn't really noticed it until you pointed it out.'

'I did?'

'You said you'd seen fish with better chins than his.'

'Oh yeah,' said Dempsey and chuckled. The chuckle turned into a roar of laughter. After a few moments Makepeace joined in.

Chapter
THIRTEEN

It took several rings of Doctor Vahimagi's doorbell before they saw a light come on in the hallway and heard approaching footsteps. Then the door opened the length of a security chain and a face peered suspiciously at them through the gap. 'Yes, what do you vant?' asked Vahimagi, a wizened gnome of a man who could have been any age between sixty and ninety.

'Hi, Doc,' said Dempsey. 'You probably don't recognise me but we met briefly once. I'm Lieutenant Dempsey.' Dempsey showed him his S.I.10 ID. Vahimagi looked at the ID, then at Dempsey. 'You're a policeman?'

'Yeah.'

'Then vy are you dressed a vaiter?'

'He's in disguise,' said Makepeace.

Vahimagi turned his attention to her and looked her up and down very slowly. 'Don't tell me — you are a policeman as well.'

'Police*woman*,' corrected Makepeace.

'Very well. A policewoman. Who is wearing what is obviously a very expensive gown which is covered in an interesting variety of stains. You are in disguise too?'

Makepeace nodded.

'Vhat as, may I ask?' said Vahimagi.

'As a jet-set bricklayer,' said Dempsey. 'Look Doc, I know we look kind of odd but this is on the level. We need your help. Urgently.' He took out the sample of concrete wrapped in his handkerchief. 'We want you to analyse this.'

'Vhat is it?'

'Concrete.'

'You know vhat time it is?'

'Yes, Doc. But it won't wait until morning.'

Vahimagi sighed. 'Very well then. Come in . . .' He unchained the door and opened it for them. 'I'm sure at least you can't be muggers. Whoever heard of muggers dressing in costumes like yours, eh?'

He led them into his study which was full of rock and mineral samples. 'Please talk quietly,' he said. My wife is upstairs asleep. She vakes and my life vill be misery for a week.'

'We won't even breathe,' Makepeace assured him.

Dempsey handed over the sample. Vahimagi went over to a microscope and put a small amount of the concrete sample on a glass slide. He bent over the eye-piece and adjusted the focus, muttering to himself in his own language. Dempsey, impatient, began to fidget . . .

'Hmmm,' said Vahimagi.

'What do you think?' asked Dempsey.

'Mmm-hmmm,' said Vahimagi.

'Soft, right?'

'Friable.'

'What?'

'It crumbles,' explained Makepeace. 'Like the cookie.'

Vahimagi looked up from his microscope. 'Did this sample come from a building?'

'Yeah,' said Dempsey. 'A bank.'

'A bank?!' exclaimed the geologist. 'How old?'

'Three years, about.'

'If you have money in this bank I suggest you move it very quickly,' said Vahimagi. He straightened, rubbed his back, then picked up another fragment of concrete and placed it in a test tube. He poured a small amount of clear liquid into the tube and swirled it around. Immediately the liquid went pink. He said, 'It came from the basement of the bank, yes?'

'Yeah,' said Dempsey. 'How'd you know?'

'Damp. Accelerates the reaction. Vhat you haf here is an Alkali-Aggregat Reaction.'

'Yeah?' said Dempsey. 'Gee . . .'

'What does that mean?' asked Makepeace.

'It means trouble,' said Vahimagi. 'It's because of the nature of the gravel used in this concrete. Do you happen to know its source?'

'I can do better than that,' Makepeace told him. She opened her purse and handed him a folded sheet of paper. 'It's an analysis report on the gravel itself.'

Vahimagi read the report and nodded. 'It is as I thought. You see, this sort of gravel is used for road beds or ballast. It is not used for concrete because it reacts with the cement.'

Dempsey said worriedly, 'You're saying that if this stuff is used in construction . . .'

'Then the construction is very unsafe. It takes

130

awhile but sooner or later . . .' Vahimagi made an 'all-fall-down' gesture with his hands.

Dempsey looked at Makepeace. 'Good God,' she whispered. 'Think of all the buildings Harris-Strang has put up using this concrete.'

Vahimagi raised his eyebrows. 'Harris-Strang? You are serious?'

'Very,' said Dempsey. 'Look, would you be willing to repeat what you've just told us in court?'

'Of course.'

'We'll be in touch with you shortly — come on, princess, let's go . . .'

In the car Dempsey said, 'So that's Harris's big secret. His buildings are unsafe. That's what he was trying to cover up.'

'But Simmons knew about it,' said Makepeace. 'And when he needed some money urgently he just popped along to a bank he knew had a vault made of weak pastry.'

'And Harris had him murdered as a result.'

'Yes. So what do we do now?'

Dempsey thought. 'Too late to do anything now. We'd better wait until morning. You lay all this on Spikings first thing. Get him to have the warrant on me withdrawn. When he's got Lacey off my back come and pick me up and we'll go pay Harris a visit. With a warrant for *his* arrest.'

She nodded. 'Right. And where will you be?'

'At the squat. Oh, and one other thing . . .'

'Yes?'

'Bring me a gun.'

Dempsey slept fitfully. He was too tense. Very soon now he would no longer be a hunted man. His life

131

could return to normal. He could go back to his apartment, shower and shave and, most importantly, *relax* again. No more constantly looking over his shoulder ...'

But first there was Harris to deal with. He couldn't wait to see the look on the fat slug's face when he and Makepeace walked into his office and arrested him for murder. That moment would make all the hassle he'd gone through during the last few days worthwhile.

He got up at 6.30 and made himself a cup of coffee. He figured Makepeace was already on her way into headquarters by now. Spikings was in the habit of arriving early. Very soon now.

The time inched by with agonising slowness. His feeling of restlessness increased. He drank more coffee and kept going to the front door, expecting to see Makepeace's car coming down the street.

By a quarter to nine he was cursing her under his breath. Where the hell had she got to? Or was Spikings being stubborn?

At nine o'clock he decided to walk to the nearest phone box — which was a couple of blocks away — and call in. He couldn't stand the waiting any longer ...

'Hi Chief. Guess who,'

'Dempsey?!'

'Yeah.'

'You've decided to give yourself up?'

'What?'

Spikings gave a long sigh. 'Come on, Lieutenant. You know this can't go on for much longer. Turn yourself in. I promise I'll back you up in court ...'

'Chief,' he broke in. 'Hasn't Makepeace given you the story yet? I thought you'd have a warrant out for Harris by now. What's the hold-up?'

'What are you talking about, Dempsey? What story?'

With an effort Dempsey stayed calm. He said, 'Is Makepeace there?'

'No. No sign of her yet.'

'She hasn't called you?'

'No. Now will you tell me what you're blathering about, Lieutenant?!'

Dempsey had a sick feeling at the pit of his stomach. And with it came a nasty suspicion. 'I'll speak to you later, Chief,' he said and hung up. He then dialled Makepeace's number. There was no answer. The nasty suspicion got nastier.

When he returned to the squat, Alison was in the kitchen. This was unusual as she and the other squat members rarely got up before noon as a rule. She frowned at him and said, 'You had a visitor.'

'Makepeace?!' he said eagerly.

'Who?'

'Blonde dame. The one who came here before.'

Alison's frown deepened and she shook her head. 'No. It was one of those motorbike courier guys. He left this for you.' She picked a brown envelope off the kitchen table and handed it to him. He saw it was addressed to 'Lieutenant James Dempsey'.

'He woke me up,' Alison said accusingly as Dempsey tore open the envelope. But Dempsey wasn't listening to her. The words on the note paper confirmed his worst fears. In stark, block letters was printed the following: IF YOU WANT TO MAKE

133

PEACE COME TO SIMMONS YARD. ALONE.

He read it through again then tore the note to pieces.

'Bad news?' asked Alison, now alarmed by the expression on his face.

'Yeah. You could say that.' He slammed his fist down on the table. Alison jumped. 'Anyone in this place got a piece?'

'A what?'

'A piece. A gun.'

She stared at him. 'Why?'

He grabbed her arm, hard. 'Look, this is important! I need a weapon. Are there any around here?'

Now looking thoroughly frightened, Alison said, 'Uhh, I think Jake's got something . . .'

'What kind of something?' Dempsey demanded, giving her a shake.

'A gun. A small one. You know he's a dealer. In speed and coke. Keeps it for self-protection.'

'Go fetch him down here. Tell him I want to borrow it. I'll make it worth his while.'

'I don't think he'll let you have . . .'

'Do as I say!' ordered Dempsey. 'Now!' He pushed her in the direction of the doorway. After giving him a fearful look she scampered out of the kitchen.

Jake appeared a short time later, dressed in a dirty dressing gown and rubbing the sleep from his eyes. Apart from Dempsey he was the oldest person in the squat. He was in his late twenties, had long greasy hair tied back in a pig-tail and an unhealthy complexion. He glared aggressively at Dempsey as he entered the kitchen with Alison following in his wake. 'Hey, man, what's all this crap about you wanting to borrow my gun?'

'It's not crap. I need a gun. Someone I know's in

134

big trouble and I'm their only chance. So give it to me, *please*!'

'You think I'm crazy? You go off with my piece and maybe use it on somebody and I end up getting the blame.' He shook his head. 'No way, man.'

'You won't get into trouble. I guarantee it.'

Jake narrowed his eyes. 'Yeah? And just how can you do that?'

'Because I'm a cop,' said Dempsey and took out his ID. Both Jake and Alison stared at it, at first disbelievingly and then with expressions of alarm. 'Jesus, he *is* a cop!' gasped Jake.

'Oh my god,' whispered Alison in a horrified tone. 'I slept with a *cop* . . . Oh my god . . .'

Jake turned suddenly. But before he could even take one step Dempsey grabbed him and slammed him against the wall. 'I asked you politely, now I'm *telling* you,' he growled. 'Give me your gun!'

Jake struggled to get free. 'Let me go, you stinking narc! You're nothing but low scum, fooling us the way you did . . .'

'I'm no narc and I don't give a damn about you and your friends, you stupid dickhead!' said Dempsey, banging him against the wall again. 'All I want from you is your gun! Get that through your thick skull before I pulp it for you! Now where is it!'

'Pocket . . .' gasped Jake as Dempsey banged his head against the wall again. 'Left hand . . . pocket . . .'

Holding him with one hand Dempsey reached down with the other. His fingers touched metal in the pocket. He drew the gun out and looked at it. It was disappointingly small. A .22 magnum Arminius. Dempsey would have preferred a heavier calibre but then, on reflection, he decided that small guns had an advantage of their own.

He let go of Jake. 'This loaded?'

'Yeah,' said Jake, eyeing him warily.

Dempsey checked. It was. He turned to Alison. 'Get me some adhesive tape. Any kind will do . . .'

She looked blank. 'What?'

'You heard me!' he bellowed. 'Move!'

She moved.

The gates leading into Simmons lumber yard were unlocked. Dempsey opened them and stepped into the yard. There were two vehicles parked there — a blue Rolls Royce and a Ford transit van. He looked around but couldn't see anyone.

He headed towards the office. He was just passing the van when he heard a voice say, 'Hold it right there, Yank. And raise your hands.' Dempsey did so then turned. Malley was emerging from behind the van. He was holding a double-barrelled shotgun. There was another man behind him. Younger, with a broad, beefy face. He was holding a Browning automatic.

'Hi, Malley,' said Dempsey cheerfully. 'How're things at the quarry? Anymore accidents?'

'Shut up, Yank. Andy, search him . . .'

While Malley kept Dempsey covered with the shotgun the younger man stepped forward and began to search him. Dempsey grinnned. 'Hello, Andy. Been in this line of work long?'

Andy scowled. He finished frisking him then stepped away. 'He's clean, Mr Malley.'

'Okay. Go and keep watch at the gates. You, Yank, go inside. But move slowly. Do anything I don't like and there's going to be nothing but a big hole where your kidneys used to be. Understand.'

136

'Yeah, I think I get the message.'

Dempsey entered the office. He wasn't surprised to see Harris behind Simmons' desk. The fat man grimaced and said, 'Sit down, Lieutenant Dempsey. Let's get this unpleasant business over as soon as we can.'

Dempsey sat down. Malley remained standing behind him. The hairs on the back of Dempsey's neck rose in response to the close proximity of the barrels of the shotgun.

'Where's Makepeace?' asked Dempsey.

Harris made a dismissive gesture with one of his pudgy hands. 'She's of no consequence at the moment. We have more important things to discuss.'

'She's the reason I'm here. I'm not saying anything to you until I know she's all right.'

'She's alive. Just how long she remains among the living depends on you,' Harris told him blandly.

'Is she all right?' Dempsey pressed.

Harris shrugged. 'We had to use a certain amount of coercion to persuade her to divulge your where-abouts but I assure you she has sustained no lasting damage.'

Dempsey struggled to keep control of his voice. 'I'm glad to hear it. Because if you're lying I'm going to kill you.'

A slight touch of colour appeared in Harris's cheeks and his lips twitched. 'You don't seem to appreciate your position, Lieutenant. You're the one with a gun pointing at the back of your head.'

'There are guns pointing at you too, Harris. Big guns.'

Harris frowned and took a quick glance out the wimdow. Dempsey laughed. 'It's okay. I was talking metaphorically. The big guns I mean are the ones that

137

are going to start firing when all those schools, hospitals and hotels you built start falling down.'

The expression in Harris's eyes grew colder. 'So you *do* know about that ...'

'So how long have you got before everything starts to fall down around your ears?'

'No guarantee that any of those buildings ever will collapse. Everyone's so bloody cautious nowadays. Surveyors, borough architects. The ones who aren't bent, that is ...' He sighed deeply. 'I got stung with that quarry, you know.'

'You want me to burst into tears?' said Dempsey.

'It's true. Some toe-rag of a land agent fixed the survey. Cost me a fortune and the stuff's useless for concrete. Bloody useless. No one does that to me.'

'So where's the agent now. In the concrete like Simmons?'

Harris shook his head. 'I wish he was. Skipped to South America. I just passed on the loss to the punters. Name of the game, old son.' As he talked his accent was changing, revealing to Dempsey his East London origins.

'When did Simmons find out you were constructing buildings out of mush?' Dempsey asked.

'He was in on it almost from the very beginning. He would have been set for life if he hadn't been so stupid — and greedy. Doing that bank was his biggest mistake. And *your* biggest mistake was sticking your nose in. Well, you were warned ...' Harris shrugged. 'My hands are clean.'

'Clean of what?'

'Your death ...' Harris gave a nod.

The back of Dempsey's head exploded.

Chapter
FOURTEEN

Dempsey woke up to find himself in the back of the transit van. His hands were tied behind him, his head throbbed horribly and he felt nauseous. But at least, he told himself, you're still alive ...

And the small .22 magnum was still taped above his inside right ankle.

It took a lot of twisting and contorting but he finally managed to reach the gun, pull it free and transfer it to the right pocket of his donkey jacket. Not long afterwards the van came to a halt then started up again, now travelling over very bumpy ground. Dempsey tried to ignore the corresponding jabs of pain that shot through his head with each bump.

The van halted again and the rear doors opened. Malley stuck his head in. 'Turn around and hold out your wrists,' he ordered. Dempsey did so and felt the ropes part as a sharp knife sliced through them. 'Play it nice and easy, Yank, and just act natural. I've got a gun in my pocket.'

That makes two of us, thought Dempsey. He climbed out of the van and discovered he was once again at the Park Palace Hotel site. Malley, his hand in his pocket, nodded towards the elevator cage. 'Get moving, Yank. And remember what I said ...'

The three of them, Dempsey, Malley and the other man, headed towards the elevator. None of the construction workers gave them a second look. Not that Dempsey minded. He wasn't ready to take any action yet. He wanted the two men on their own — and he guessed that was their intention too. In a way it was an amusing situation but he didn't feel like laughing. He was too worried about Makepeace.

They got into the cage. 'Taking me for a ride, are you, Malley?'

'Shut up,' growled Malley as he pushed the UP button.

'Not too happy, are you, Malley?' continued Dempsey. 'Idea of topping a copper doesn't appeal to you, does it?'

'I told you to shut up.' He pushed outwards with the gun in his pocket so that Dempsey could see the outline of the barrel through the cloth.

'Don't be stupid,' said Dempsey calmly. 'You can't shoot me. It's got to look like an accident, right?'

'If you don't keep your mouth shut I'll use *this* on you!' From his other pocket he took out a blackjack.

'You've already used that on me. In fact, that's twice you've hit me over the head, Malley. I owe you.'

'Yeah, well where you're going it's kind of difficult to settle debts ...'

'There are ways,' Dempsey told him and smiled.

The rest of the journey up the side of the skeletal

structure was made in silence. On some levels they passed welders at work but the top level, Dempsey saw when they arrived, was deserted.

'Out,' ordered Malley.

'It's okay. I know the way,' said Dempsey. 'I've been here before.'

They walked along the narrow catwalk to the rear of the building. When they reached a wooden platform extending out from the scaffolding Malley told him to halt. But instead Dempsey walked to the edge and calmly leant over the single beam of wood that acted as a barrier, 'Nice view. On a clear day I bet you can see Wormwood Scrubs from here.' Then he turned and faced Malley and the other man. 'But a bit too cold for me.' He thrust his hands deep into the pockets of his donkey jacket and hunched up his shoulders, pretending to shiver.

'Don't worry, you won't be cold much longer,' said Malley with a sneer. He took the gun out of his pocket. Dempsey recognised it. It was Makepeace's .32 revolver. 'Turn around again,' ordered Malley.

Dempsey didn't move. 'First you answer me a question. Where's Makepeace?'

'In storage,' Malley said and grinned.

'You going to kill her too?'

'Me? No way.'

'But someone is?'

Malley shook his head. 'Nah. No need to. Nature is just going to take its course. Right, Andy?'

'Yeah,' said Andy. 'I guess.' He didn't seem too sure.

'Enough of the chit-chat,' said Malley. 'Turn around, Dempsey. Time for you to take your giant step for mankind. But don't worry — I'll help you make the take-off with this ...' He took the black-

141

jack out of his pocket again.

Dempsey still didn't turn. 'One last time — where's Makepeace?'

'Turn *around*, I said!' Malley yelled, raising the .32.

Dempsey fired through the pocket of his jacket. The muffled .22 made a sound like a cap pistol. The bullet hit Malley in the upper chest. He frowned then looked down at the small hole in the thick cloth of his jacket. Dempsey quickly drew the .22 out of his pocket. Such a small calibre weapon was practically useless against a man of Malley's bulk unless you hit him in the right place ...

As Malley looked up again, the realization of what had happened to him dawning in his eyes, Dempsey fired again. This time a small, deceptively neat hole appeared in Malley's forehead, just above his left eyebrow.

Malley's mouth dropped open in surprise and he fell backwards. All this had taken just a few seconds. Dempsey turned his attention to the younger man who was desperately trying to pull the Browning out of his pocket but, in his panic, had snagged it.

'Freeze!' ordered Dempsey. 'Don't make me shoot!'

But he kept tugging on the gun and when Dempsey saw it start to come free he had no choice. Dempsey's .22 made its childish sound three times.

Then Dempsey sighed and walked over to where the man lay groaning on the platform. He'd hoped he'd merely wounded him but one look at the blood running from the corner of his mouth told Dempsey otherwise. 'I warned you, buddy,' said Dempsey, bending over him. The younger man's eyes were round with fear and he grabbed convulsively at

Dempsey's sleeve. He coughed and gasped, 'Help me
... I don't want to die ...'

'I'll get you a doctor,' said Dempsey even though
he knew it would be no use. 'But before I do I want to
know where Makepeace is ...'

The man coughed again and from the sound he
made Dempsey knew he was rapidly drowning in his
own blood. 'Don't ... want ... to ... die ... please ...'

'Well, you will if you don't tell me where Makepeace is,' said Dempsey brutally.

'She's ... she's ...' His voice faded. Dempsey put
his ear to the dying man's mouth. 'Talk, damn you!'

'In ... she's in Simmons' yard ...' These words
were followed by another bout of coughing. More
blood bubbled out of his mouth and his eyes rolled
back in their sockets. Dempsey prised his dead fingers
from his sleeve, pocketed the Browning and stood up.

He walked over to Malley. 'You won't be needing
this either,' he said as he bent down and picked up
Makepeace's revolver. 'By the way, I'll give your
regards to your boss.'

Dempsey solved the problem of transport by stealing
a car belonging to one of the construction workers.
He figured that becoming a car thief was small beer
for someone on the run for murder. Besides, Makepeace's life was at stake ...

By some miracle he reached Simmons' yard without having a traffic accident or being stopped for
speeding. The gates to the yard were locked this time
but he simply drove straight at them. The impact
snapped the chain and the gates flew open.

He braked with a screech of rubber outside the
office and jumped out of the car, which now had a

large dent in its front. Dempsey drew the Browning and ran to the office entrance. There were no other vehicles in the yard but that didn't mean Harris hadn't left one or more of his men around to guard Makepeace ...

Providing she was still alive ...

He blocked that thought from his mind.

He tried the office door. It too was locked. He kicked it open and entered warily, gun at the ready. The place was in silence. He quickly checked through the small building. It was empty.

Dempsey went back outside into the yard and searched the storage sheds. He looked behind every stack of lumber and carefully examined every inch of floor surface looking for trapdoors.

At the end of two hours he was ready to admit defeat. If Makepeace was hidden somewhere in the yard it was one hell of a hiding place ...

He ran Malley's words through his mind again. '... In storage ... Nature is just going to take its course ...'

God, thought Dempsey, had they *buried* her? He hastily examined the yard for signs of freshly turned earth but couldn't see any.

Stumped, he returned to the office and sat down at Simmons' desk. He had the terrible feeling that time was rapidly running out for Makepeace but there was nothing he could do. He had run out of places to look ...

Had the dying man lied? No, it was doubtful. He'd been too scared. Then where was she? Had Harris come back and moved her to another location?

Burning with frustration, Dempsey began to tap his foot restlessly on the floor ... and heard something rattle. He frowned, looking under the desk.

There was a metal handle by his foot.

He leapt up and shoved the large desk to one side as if it weighed nothing. The trapdoor lay fully exposed. Dempsey yanked it open to reveal a set of steps leading down into the darkness. 'Makepeace!' he yelled but there was no answer.

Frantically he hunted around the office until he found a flashlight then he climbed down through the trapdoor.

Almost immediately he experienced a crushing disappointment. Apart from a few crates and cardboard boxes the basement was empty. He checked the crates but they contained nothing but rusting bits of machinery. 'Shit,' he muttered and sat down on one of the crates. He'd been so *sure* . . .

Idly he swung the beam of the flashlight around the walls. Then he noticed something. The far wall was a darker colour than the other three. He got up and went over to it. It looked new. He touched it. It was damp . . .

He rushed back upstairs and hunted round the yard until he located what he needed — a sledge-hammer and a crowbar. He returned to the wall and attacked it with the sledge-hammer. The fresh concrete crumbled under his blows. Very soon he'd dug an eighteen inch deep hole in it. Six inches further and the head of the hammer penetrated through to an open space. He put his mouth to the hole and yelled Makepeace's name. No answer. Then he shone the flashlight through it and saw another, older, wall about two and half feet further away. He tried to see what lay at the bottom of the gap between the two walls but his field of vision was too restricted. He had to make the hole bigger.

Using the crowbar he widened the cavity until he could get his head and shoulders into it then he looked again.

At the bottom of the narrow space lay Makepeace. She was bound and gagged. Her eyes were closed and she didn't appear to be breathing.

Chapter
FIFTEEN

Dempsey went berserk. The concrete collapsed under his onslaught and within a brief amount of time he was able to drag Makepeace out of her makeshift coffin.

He pulled the gag from her mouth and put his cheek close to her lips. This confirmed the horrible truth. She wasn't breathing . . .

He put his mouth on hers and blew air into her lungs. Then he took a deep breath and repeated the process. Again and again.

He lost all track of time. He was giving way to despair when, just as he was turning his head to take in another breath, he heard a weak but indignant voice say, 'Dempsey, what on *earth* do you think you're doing?'

Dempsey looked at her and started to laugh.

After he'd untied her and massaged her wrists and ankles until the blood started circulating again he asked her what had happened.

'They were waiting in my car park when I got back last night,' she told him, her voice still weak. 'They brought me here. Harris wanted to know where you were hiding out. I refused to tell him so he ...' She faltered.

'Go on, princess.'

'He ... he had that ape-man of his, Malley, do some tricks with a lighted cigarette.' She looked away. 'I'm sorry, Dempsey. I gave them the address ...'

He patted her hand. 'Hey, no sweat, princess. Torture's my weak point too. I'd have done the same as you.'

'Yes?' she said bitterly. 'I doubt it.' Then she said, 'I want that creep. He's going to pay a long time for what he did ...'

'Malley? You're too late. He's out of the game.'

She looked at him. 'He's dead?'

'Yeah. The other guy too.'

'What happened?'

Dempsey told her. She nodded with satisfaction. 'Now let's go pay Harris a visit.' She got to her feet, swaying unsteadily.

'Whoa, princess,' said Dempsey, grabbing her to prevent her from falling. 'You're in no condition to go anywhere but hospital. Leave Harris to me.'

She shook her head. 'Nope. I insist on coming with you. I'll be fine as soon as I can get some fresh air. Really.'

'Who are you trying to kid? You're half-dead ...'

'Dempsey, I'm not going to argue with you. I *have* to be there when Harris is arrested. Do you understand?'

148

He saw the expression in her eyes and nodded. 'Yeah. I do.' He reached into his pocket and took out the .32. 'Here, I think this belongs to you ...'

Both the Harris-Strang receptionists gave a start of surprise when they saw Dempsey and Makepeace striding towards them. What they saw were two grim-faced, dust-covered apparitions who looked like survivors of some terrible earthquake.

'Hello again,' said Dempsey, grinning unpleasantly down at them. 'We're here to see Mr Harris.' He flashed his ID. 'Please don't announce us. We'd like to surprise him.'

'But wait! You can't ...!' cried one of the girls as Dempsey and Makepeace swept past the desk and started to head down the corridor that led to Harris's office. They ignored her and kept going.

As they turned the first corner they saw a security man approaching them at a run, a walkie-talkie in his hand. 'Stop right there!' he ordered. But they kept walking at the same pace. Then Dempsey hit him, hard. The security man doubled over, clutching his stomach and struggling to breathe. Dempsey lowered him gently to the floor. 'Sorry, pal, but we don't have the time for small talk ...'

When they burst into Harris's outer office the glacial secretary was talking on the phone. Her eyes widened with alarm and she said into the phone, 'Yes, they're here now. Call the ...' Dempsey grabbed the phone from her hand. 'Call the what?' he demanded. 'Tell me or I'll go fetch another fire extinguisher.'

She swallowed nervously. 'The ... Divisional Commander ...' she said.

'Interesting,' murmured Dempsey. Then he said

into the mouthpiece, 'Do as she said, darling, call the Divisional Commander.' Then he hung up and drew the Browning automatic. 'Let's go!' he said to Makepeace.

He threw open the sliding doors that led into Harris's office and stepped inside, followed by Makepeace. Harris, seated at his desk, stared disbelievingly at them. His pasty face went whiter. 'You ...?' he gasped. 'How ...?' But then he recovered his self-control and the familiar bland mask was back in position on his face. He even managed a bleak smile at Dempsey. 'Persistent bastard, aren't you?'

'You'd better believe it, fatso,' Dempsey told him.

Harris glanced at Makepeace. 'It's quite a surprise seeing you again too, my dear. I was under the impression your disappearance would become one of the great unsolved mysteries of our time. How on earth did you escape? I'm really intrigued to know.'

Makepeace said, 'You should be aware by now that your concrete can't be relied upon for anything.'

He pursed his lips. 'Er, look, about that unpleasantness earlier today. It was all most regrettable — and quite avoidable if you'd only been more cooperative. I must admit, though, that Malley did get carried away.' He turned to Dempsey. 'And where is Malley, may I ask?'

'He's left your employ. I made him redundant.'

Harris nodded. 'I see. Pity. You'd be surprised at how hard it is to find reliable killers.'

'Yeah, well, we've all got our problems. And your biggest problem right now is a twenty year jail sentence. But don't worry, we'll find you a jail you didn't build yourself.'

There was a noise in the outer office. Dempsey glanced back and saw several security men rushing through the door. 'Hold it!' he ordered, raising the automatic and pointing it at Harris's head. 'One more step and your boss will need a brain transplant.'

The security men halted and looked questioningly at Harris. 'Do as he says. It's all right. No doubt the police are on their way.'

'Yeah, they are,' agreed Dempsey. 'But they'll be taking you away, fatso, not us. Can't you get it through your skull yet? You're finished. It's all over for you.'

Harris shook his football of a head. 'No it's not. I'm not finished by a long shot. I've got influence. Powerful friends. I'm even in line for a knighthood. What are you two compared to me? Nothing but a pair of stupid policemen ...'

'Actually, one of us is a police *woman*,' said Makepeace.

'And we're not so stupid as someone who goes around building hospitals and schools out of cheesy concrete.' Dempsey turned to the group of watching security men. 'You hear that? It's true. The guy you work for is going to become a mass-murderer any day now.'

'Don't believe a word of it,' Harris told them calmly. 'He's mad. They both are.'

There was another commotion in the outer office. This time it marked the arrival of Lacey ...

'Drop that gun, Dempsey!' ordered Lacey as he pushed his way through the security men. He was followed by Taylor and three uniformed officers. 'I warn you we're armed!'

A glance told Dempsey this was true. But he kept the Browning aimed at Harris's head. 'Hi Lacey,' Dempsey said cheerily. 'Glad you could make it. You're just in time to see Makepeace and me arrest

151

Harris. For Murder, Conspiracy to Murder and Conspiracy to Pervert the Course of Justice, to name but a few.'

'You're insane, Dempsey,' Lacey told him. He looked at Makepeace. 'What about you, Sergeant? Where do you stand in all this?'

Makepeace drew her .32 and pointed it at Harris. 'I'm with Dempsey. All the way. Everything he says is true. Harris has been putting up buildings using bad cement. It's to do with the gravel from his quarry. It's no good. And we can get a sworn statement from an expert who's analysed the stuff to back us up.'

'She's lying, Detective Chief Inspector,' said Harris. 'It's all nonsense.'

'That's why Harris had Simmons killed,' continued Makepeace. 'Simmons robbed that bank because he knew the concrete vault might as well have been made of cardboard. By doing so he put Harris and his whole operation in jeopardy — so he was murdered. And when Dempsey became suspicious Harris had him framed for the murder.'

'I don't believe any of this,' protested Lacey. 'It's ridiculous. A man in Mr Harris's position . . .'

'Yeah,' nodded Dempsey. 'I appreciate your problem. After all, Harris has the ear of your Divisional Commander. Hopkins, right? They're real buddy-buddy together. And if Harris speaks, Hopkins hops. He's the reason both you and Spikings put pressure on me to drop the Simmons case. Am I right?'

Lacey didn't answer. Dempsey glanced at him. For the first time ever he saw an expression of doubt on Lacey's face. 'Yeah, I thought so,' said Dempsey with satisfaction. 'And the reason is that Hopkins is in Harris's pocket.'

'That's preposterous!' spluttered Lacey. 'Divisional

Commander Hopkins has an exemplary police record! To suggest that he takes bribes is unthinkable!'

'I'll do more than suggest it,' Dempsey said. 'I'll accuse him of it in court. Am I right, Harris?'

Harris's complexion was no longer white. It had gone a distinct shade of grey. Then, abruptly, his shoulders slumped.

'Am I right, Harris?' repeated Dempsey.

Harris didn't answer but just stared vacantly into space. Then, after several moments of silence, he made a long sighing sound — like a tyre deflating — and stood up. 'Don't try anything stupid, Harris,' Dempsey warned him.

But Harris simply turned his back on everyone and stared out through his huge window. He sighed again and said, 'You can't quite see it from here but I started down there, in Wandsworth — five bob an hour, digging up roads for the Council. I've come a long way ... a long, long way since that time. And now, just because of a few yards of iffy concrete I'm going to be a nothing again ...'

'Mr Harris! Are you saying there's some *truth* in all this?' cried Lacey in a shocked voice.

Harris ignored him. He started to speak again but it was as if he was speaking to himself. 'I like high places. Always have done. I like looking down on people. Makes you feel good being up high. Sometimes when I look out here I think I could just ...' He took three steps back from the window. Then he lowered his head and, like a bull, charged ...

He hit the glass with a loud *crack*. The impact of his heavy body sent long fractures across the thick window but the glass didn't shatter. Harris staggered back then charged again.

But by this time Dempsey had dashed forward.

Dropping his gun he grabbed the back of Harris's jacket with both hands and hauled him back. Harris lost his balance and fell backward to the floor with a thud. There was blood on his face from a long gash in his scalp but Dempsey could see he wasn't badly hurt.

He turned to Lacey who looked as stunned as the prone Harris. 'He's all yours, sheriff.' Dempsey picked up the Browning and handed it to him. 'Belonged to one of his men. I wouldn't be surprised if it didn't turn out to be the same gun that killed Phelps.'

Lacey stared wordlessly at the gun in his hand then back at Dempsey. He opened his mouth to say something but no sounds came out. Dempsey gave him a reassuring pat on the shoulder. 'Yeah, I know it's all kind of taken you by surprise but I'll make sure you get a copy of our report later. Right now me and the little lady are going to ride off into the sunset together.' He went and took Makepeace by the arm. 'Come on, Calamity. Now that we've cleaned up this here town it's time we hit the trail.'

As he led her through the silent crowd of security men and police officers she leaned over and whispered in his ear, 'Actually, I'm ready for that trip to the hospital now. I think I'm going to pass out . . .'

'Hang on just a little longer, princess,' he whispered back. 'This scene is gonna make us legends in every police canteen across the country.'

Chapter

SIXTEEN

There was a hesitant tap at the door of Makepeace's hospital room. She exchanged a glance with Dempsey who, once again clean-shaven and wearing a neatly-pressed suit, was sitting beside her bed and eating his way through the box of chocolates he'd bought her. 'Another visitor,' he said, chewing. 'You're more popular than I thought.'

'Come in,' Makepeace called out. The door opened and Spikings entered with a bunch of roses in his hand and a sheepish look on his face. 'Er, hello, Sergeant,' he said in an unusually subdued voice as he approached the bed. 'How are you?'

'I'm fine. They're letting me leave tomorrow.'

Spikings handed her the flowers and stood there looking uncomfortable. 'You want me to go get you a chair?' asked Dempsey.

'No, no, that won't be necessary. I won't be staying long. Just dropped in to see how Makepeace was and to ... well, to apologise. To you both, in fact.'

Dempsey and Makepeace exchanged another glance.

'I was wrong and you were ... were right,' said Spikings, with obvious difficulty. 'I should have listened. And I shouldn't have let myself be pressured by Hopkins.'

After an awkward silence Dempsey said diplomatically, 'Hey, forget it, Chief. We all make mistakes. So what's happening with Hopkins anyway?'

'He's confessed to everything. There's going to be a big enquiry. Apparently the relationship with Harris goes back some years and there may be others involved.'

'Like Lacey?' asked Dempsey hopefully.

'No. He's clean. Squeaky clean, in fact. All this has come as a tremendous shock to him. He thought very highly of Hopkins. He's been put on leave until he recovers ...'

Dempsey laughed. Spikings glowered at him.

'What about Harris?' asked Makepeace quickly.

'He's been talking non-stop too. Lot of interesting stuff coming out. Seems he's been involved in other murders apart from Simmons and Phelps. Five of them over the years. Business rivals, stroppy trucking contractors and the like ...'

'Nice guy,' said Dempsey. 'Good thing we found out before he got his knighthood. Could have been real embarrassing, right?'

Spikings gave him another dirty look. 'Of course, the main concern at the moment are all those dodgy buildings of his. They're going beserk at the Department of the Environment. Got experts running around taking samples to check the rate of the deterioration. There's talk at least two schools may have to be evacuated immediately.'

'I hope this hospital wasn't a Harris-Strang project,' said Makepeace.

'No. Not on the list,' Spikings assured her. Then he stared uncomfortably at his feet for a time before saying gruffly, 'I don't need to tell you that if it hadn't been for you two we could have had a major disaster on our hands. *Several* major disasters, in fact. Needless to say, there will be an official recognition of your efforts . . .'

'You mean we're gonna get a reward?' asked Dempsey, looking pleased.

'More like a medal each,' Makepeace told him. 'This isn't America.'

'A medal each, yes,' agreed Spikings. 'And a trip to the Palace is also on the cards.'

'The Palace?' frowned Dempsey. 'What's that? A nightclub? Or a restaurant?'

'*The* Palace, Dempsey,' said Spikings. 'Buckingham Palace.'

'Yeah?' Dempsey grinned. 'Hey, you mean I get to meet Chuck and Di again?'

Spikings looked mystified. 'What do you mean *again?*'

'Don't ask,' said Makepeace, and shuddered at the memory.

Spikings glanced at them both then shook his head. 'Well, I must be going. Lot of work waiting for me back at headquarters what with Chas still away on his honeymoon and you two on leave . . .' He gave Makepeace a quick smile. 'Take care of yourself, Sergeant.'

When he'd gone Makepeace said, 'Well, I've never seen him like *that* before.'

'Yeah, he was almost human.'

'I hope it's just a temporary condition. I'd find it too eerie for words if he was like that all the time.'

'Yeah.' Dempsey glanced at his watch. 'Hey, I gotta be going as well.'

'You might as well. You've finished all the chocolates you bought me.'

He leaned over and gave her a kiss on the cheek. 'I'll bring you some more later. Right now I got to go pay a visit to that squat I was staying at and return a couple of favours to some people there.'

'They won't recognise you the way you look now.'

He sighed. 'Yeah. I'm a cop again.'

'What's it feel like?'

He grinned at her. 'Good. Real good.'

As he stepped into the corridor he saw, in the distance, the approaching figure of the Honourable Nigel Penward. He was carrying an enormous bunch of flowers and what appeared to be a Harrods gift hamper.

Dempsey quickly ducked back into Makepeace's room. 'Princess, I was just thinking — you want I should get in contact with Lord Flaunt-it-all and tell him you're here?'

She shook her head firmly. 'I never want to see that creep again.'

'Got the message,' he said, and withdrew. He intercepted Penward some yards down the corridor from Makepeace's room. 'Just a second, bud,' he said, blocking Penward's way. 'Where do you think you're going?'

Penward frowned at him. 'Oh, it's *you*. For a moment I didn't recognise you without your usual layer of dirt.'

'I asked you where you think you're going.'

'It's none of your business but I'm going to visit Harriet. I just learned from her father that she was a patient here.'

'She doesn't want to see you,' said Dempsey. 'Shove off.'

Penward's face darkened. 'Who the hell do you think you are?! If I want to see Harriet I will! You can't stop me!'

'Want to bet?' challenged Dempsey.

'Yes, I do!' Penward turned and thrust the flowers and hamper into the arms of a passing nurse. 'Here, girl, hold these a moment.'

The startled nurse tried to protest but Penward was already turning back to face Dempsey, his fists raised. 'I'm going to thrash the life out of you, you boorish, thick-headed *Yank*!'

Dempsey sighed and punched him quickly on the jaw. Penward fell backwards. Dempsey waited for him to get up again but he didn't move. Then he saw that he was out cold. 'Better get someone to take him to Casualty,' Dempsey told the shocked nurse. 'Oh, and you can keep that hamper yourself. Share it out among the other nurses. He'd like that.'

As Dempsey strode off, whistling, down the corridor, he massaged the knuckles of his right hand and said to himself, 'I was right. The guy *did* have a weak chin.'

159

All Futura Books are available at your bookshop or newsagent, or can be ordered from the following address:
Futura Books, Cash Sales Department,
P.O. Box 11, Falmouth, Cornwall

Please send cheque or postal order (no currency), and allow 55p for postage and packing for the first book plus 22p for the second book and 14p for each additional book ordered up to a maximum charge of £1.75 in U.K.

Customers in Eire and B.F.P.O. please allow 55p for the first book, 22p for the second book plus 14p per copy for the next 7 books, thereafter 8p per book.

Overseas customers please allow £1.00 for postage and packing for the first book and 25p per copy for each additional book.